The First Time I Saw Him

Also by Laura Dave

London is the Best City in America
The Divorce Party
The First Husband
Eight Hundred Grapes
Hello, Sunshine
The Last Thing He Told Me
The Night We Lost Him

The First Time I Saw Him

LAURA DAVE

CENTURY

CENTURY

UK | USA | Canada | Ireland | Australia
India | New Zealand | South Africa

Century is part of the Penguin Random House group of companies whose addresses can be found at global.penguinrandomhouse.com

Penguin Random House UK,
One Embassy Gardens, 8 Viaduct Gardens, London SW11 7BW

penguin.co.uk
global.penguinrandomhouse.com

First published in the US by Simon & Schuster 2026
First published in the UK by Century 2026
001

Copyright © Laura Dave, 2026

The moral right of the author has been asserted

Penguin Random House values and supports copyright. Copyright fuels creativity, encourages diverse voices, promotes freedom of expression and supports a vibrant culture. Thank you for purchasing an authorised edition of this book and for respecting intellectual property laws by not reproducing, scanning or distributing any part of it by any means without permission. You are supporting authors and enabling Penguin Random House to continue to publish books for everyone. No part of this book may be used or reproduced in any manner for the purpose of training artificial intelligence technologies or systems. In accordance with Article 4(3) of the DSM Directive 2019/790, Penguin Random House expressly reserves this work from the text and data mining exception.

Printed and bound in Great Britain by Clays Ltd, Elcograf S.p.A.

The authorised representative in the EEA is Penguin Random House Ireland, Morrison Chambers, 32 Nassau Street, Dublin D02 YH68

A CIP catalogue record for this book is available from the British Library

ISBN: 978–1–529–91206–7 (hardback)
ISBN: 978–1–529–91207–4 (trade paperback)

Penguin Random House is committed to a sustainable future for our business, our readers and our planet. This book is made from Forest Stewardship Council® certified paper.

For Josh,
The first time I saw you I knew

Maybe, one day,
we'll bump into each other,
in a checkout line or a quiet car lot,
and we'll smile like we didn't
shatter each other once—
like we didn't make an unholy
mess of love.

—Harriet Selina

The First Time I Saw Him

Prologue

I'm at the Pacific Design Center in Los Angeles, participating in a First Look exhibition, with twenty-one other artisans and producers. I'm debuting a new collection of white oak pieces (mostly furniture, a few bowls and smaller pieces) in the showroom they've provided.

These exhibitions are great for exposure to potential clients, but they are also like a reunion of sorts—and, like most reunions, somewhat of a grind. Several architects and colleagues stop by to say hello, catch up. I have done my best with the small talk, but I'm starting to feel tired. And, as the clock winds toward 6 p.m., I feel myself looking past people as opposed to at them.

Bailey is supposed to meet me for dinner, so I'm mostly on the lookout for her, excited to have the excuse to shut it all down for the day. She is bringing a guy she recently started dating, a hedge funder named Shep (two points against him), but she swears I'll like him. *He's not like that*, she says.

I'm not sure if she is referring to him working in finance or having the name Shep. Either way, he seems like a reaction to her last boyfriend, who had a less irritating name (John) and was unemployed. So it is, dating in your twenties, and I'm grateful that these are the things she's thinking about.

She lives in Los Angeles now. I live here too, not too far from the ocean—and not too far from her.

I sold the floating house as soon as Bailey graduated high school.

I don't harbor any illusions that this means I've avoided them keeping tabs on us—the shadowy figures waiting to pounce should Owen ever return. I'm sure they are still watching on the off chance he risks it and comes back to see us. I operate as if they are always watching, whether or not he does.

Sometimes I think I see them, in an airport lounge or outside a restaurant, but of course I don't know who they are. I profile anyone who looks at me a second too long. It stops me from letting too many people get close to me, which isn't a bad thing. I have who I need.

Minus one.

He walks into the showroom, casually, a backpack over his shoulders. His shaggy hair is buzz cut short and darker, and his nose is crooked, like it's been broken. He wears a button-down shirt, rolled up, revealing a sleeve of tattoos, crawling out to his hand, to his fingers, like a spider.

This is when I clock his wedding ring, which he is still wearing. The ring I made for him. Its slim oak finish is perhaps unnoticeable to anyone else. I know it cold though. He couldn't look less like himself. There is that too. But maybe this is what you do when you need to hide from people in plain sight. I wonder. Then I wonder if it isn't him, after all.

It isn't the first time I think I see him. I think I see him everywhere.

I'm so flustered that I drop the papers I'm holding, everything falling to the floor.

He bends over to help me. He doesn't smile, which would give him away. He doesn't so much as touch my hand. It would be too much, probably, for both of us.

He hands me the papers.

I try and thank him. Do I say it out loud? I don't know.

Maybe. Because he nods.

The First Time I Saw Him

Then he stands up and starts to head out, the way he came. And it's then that he says the one thing that only he would say to me.

"The could have been boys still love you," Owen says. He isn't looking at me when he says it, his voice low.

The way you say hello.

The way you say goodbye.

My skin starts burning, my cheeks flaring red. But I don't say anything. There's no time to say anything. He shrugs and shifts his backpack higher on his shoulder. Then he disappears into the crowd. And that's that. He is just another design junkie, on his way to another booth.

I don't dare watch him go. I don't dare look in his direction.

I keep my eyes down, pretending to organize the papers, but the heat coming off me is tangible—that fierce red lingering on my skin, on my face, if anyone is paying close enough attention in that moment. I pray they are not.

I make myself count to a hundred, then to a hundred and fifty.

When I finally allow myself to look up, it's Bailey that I see. It cools me out immediately, centers me. She is walking toward me from the same direction Owen has gone. She's in her gray sweater dress and high-top Converse, her long, brown hair running halfway down her back. Did Owen pass her? Did he get to see for himself how beautiful she has become? How sure of herself? I hope so. I hope so at the same time I hope not. Which way, after all, spares him?

I take a deep breath and take her in. She walks hand in hand with Shep, the new boyfriend. He gives me a salute, which I'm sure he thinks is cute. It isn't.

But I smile as they walk up. How can I not? Bailey is smiling too. She is smiling at me.

"Mom," she says.

Part I

For whatever we lose (like a you or a me)
It's always ourselves we find in the sea

—e. e. cummings

If You Can Forgive Me . . .

On the way out of the Pacific Design Center, Owen passes her.

This is the first time he has laid eyes on his daughter in person in more than five years. Five years, ten months, and twenty-four days— to be exact. Five birthdays and five Christmases and eight performances (*Wicked* and *Carousel* and *Spring Awakening* and *Dear Evan Hanson* and *Waitress* and *Beautiful* and *Chicago* and *Carousel* again) and two graduations (one high school, one college) and three new addresses and a summer in Williamstown, Massachusetts, and the start of her first job. All these things between sixteen and twenty-two that mark it up, the start of a life.

Bailey's hair is longer, her arms too thin. But, at the moment he passes her—he doesn't turn to take a longer look; he won't allow himself that luxury—it's her skin that gets him.

Bailey is tan, if her skin were capable of tanning, her skin freckled and reddish, perhaps from the daily toll of life in Southern California, perhaps from spending too many days at the beach. How is this possible? Hadn't she always avoided the beach? It nearly breaks him, such a small and obvious difference in who his daughter has become.

Seeing Bailey online didn't give this away. Seeing Bailey online was a completely different thing.

Her social media account is now public, which Owen tells himself she's done for his benefit. He wouldn't allow her to ever post photos before, but the rules are different now. Owen imagines that Bailey knows this. There is no asking her. Either way, he likes to believe the posts are a way of keeping them in conversation. All he needs is a public computer and her handle and he can go to her page with no record of having gone there. Her smile (how he loved every single thing about his kid's smile) knocks the wind out of him, each and every time. It's almost like it's directed at him: *Look, Dad, I'm okay. Look, Dad, you're not here. Look, Dad, I'll never forgive you.*

Owen walks through the design center lobby, out the revolving doors, and onto Melrose. There is a line of taxis idling. The driver in the first taxi shakes his head, still in the middle of a dinner break. So Owen gets into the second cab and asks the driver to take him to the airport. They are fighting early-evening Los Angeles traffic and it takes longer than expected to get there. It doesn't matter. He is plenty early for his flight and heads to the first-class lounge, flashes his mobile boarding pass, and goes into a single bathroom, where he locks the door.

He stares at himself in the mirror, takes his first deep breath. Steadies himself. Then he starts to take his clothes off. He strips off the button-down shirt he was wearing, puts on a plain T-shirt and leather jacket, swaps his combat boots for a pair of Converse sneakers. Just like his kid's.

On the way to the lounge's bar, he sees a janitor with her large garbage bin and tosses his old clothes inside. Then he takes a seat on the corner barstool, the farthest stool from anyone else, taking out a novel he has no intention of reading.

The bartender puts a wine list down in front of Owen. "What can I get you to drink?" he asks.

"Whatever red you're pouring is fine."

"That's a mistake," a woman says.

Owen looks up, sees the woman at the other end of the bar,

The First Time I Saw Him

smiling at him. She is pretty, with a short pixie cut, tortoiseshell glasses.

"Sorry?" he says.

"The wine. It's a mistake. My flight's delayed. Very delayed. So I've been working my way down the list of wines by the glass. They're all bad."

He opens his novel, tries to close off whatever conversation she wants to have.

But she moves down the bar, so she's two stools away from him. "So where are you headed?"

"Business trip," he says.

"International?"

He's not surprised she guesses international. His New Zealand passport is sticking out of his book, complete with a name that doesn't belong to him.

The bartender puts down the glass of wine in front of him along with a bowl of salty nuts. Owen nods a thank-you, takes a sip.

"Awful, isn't it?"

"It'll do."

He offers a quick smile, turns back to his book.

"Should we try our luck at a bottle instead?"

"The thing is . . ." he says. "I'm married."

She looks down at his hand, eyes his wedding band. "And what does that have to do with splitting a bottle of wine?"

But then she shrugs, as if to say she knows exactly what that has to do with it.

"Just trying to avoid any confusion," Owen says.

"Lucky woman then. Your wife."

He thinks of Hannah. He hasn't allowed himself to think of her, not since leaving the design center. Not since he was bending down next to her on the floor, helping pick up those scattered papers. Her hand so near to his hand. Her hair against his face. Her eyes giving her away, like they always had. There was anger there. And confusion. And love. Was there still love beneath the rest?

He smiles. "Not sure that she would say that."

"What would she say? Your wife?"

"I ask myself that all the time."

~

Here's the thing.

You don't know what you will do until you do it. You pick up the phone at work and it's your wife's best friend and she tells you to go someplace where no one else can hear you and you close the conference room door and she starts to speak (*The FBI is on the way, The Shop is being raided*) and your whole world changes.

Just like that.

It's been five years. More than five years. Owen can't recall—not with exact accuracy—what he said to Jules on that call, or how he got off the phone with her.

He just remembers the movement, which started immediately. The only goal was to get out of there before the FBI arrived. To get far away from there before anyone could attempt to ID him. There was a yellow legal pad on his desk. He picked it up and tossed it into his messenger bag and headed out of the office.

Early lunch? the receptionist asked. Owen nodded. He knows that he nodded. He knows that he hid his urgency the best that he could. His urgency, his fear. *I'll be back in a little while,* he said. *See you later . . .*

Then he was out the front doors and racing through the parking lot and keying the lock to his car.

The First Time I Saw Him

He got in and drove to the bank in Corte Madera, to the oldest bank in Corte Madera, which housed an underground vault with three bottom-row safe-deposit boxes under a numbered account.

He took a duffel bag and a messenger bag out of his trunk—the two bags he'd kept stored in his trunk precisely for this moment—and brought them inside the bank with him. Inside the vault.

Two safe-deposit boxes held the money. He filled up the duffel bag with all of it. The third deposit box had a Canadian passport, two drivers' licenses, an iPhone with an encrypted phone app already downloaded and connected, and a key to a storage unit in Vancouver. These he put into his messenger bag.

Before he walked out, on the floor of that vault, he wrote his daughter a note and put it in the duffel bag.

Then, he wrote his wife a note and put it in his back pocket.

He didn't go to the docks. There was no time to go to the docks. And even if there were, he wouldn't go. If he saw Hannah, he wouldn't have been able to leave without telling her everything. He couldn't tell her everything, not if he wanted to keep her safe. He couldn't tell her anything. He needed to be in Vancouver by the next day.

He drove through the night. He drove for thirteen hours straight, stopping only twice. Fifteen minutes per stop—once at a rest stop in Astoria, Oregon, the second time at Lumen Field in Seattle, where he left his car at the rear of the eight-story parking structure. He walked from Lumen Field to the nearby Greyhound bus station, where he hopped a bus to take him the rest of the way over the border into Canada.

But first he went to his daughter's school and put the duffel bag in her locker, and found a girl leaving soccer practice, and handed her the note for Hannah. First, he said a prayer that they wouldn't hate him for this. Not his daughter, not his wife.

But it was the wrong prayer. The right prayer was closer to the second one he made as he crossed the border into Canada: He prayed they'd understand.

They'd understand that he did have an escape hatch ready—for years he had it ready—one that included them.

But he'd planned it when Bailey was still a child, before his daughter became so specifically herself that to ask her to run felt more selfish than safe. It was before Owen understood what it would do to his wife, how it would blow an impossible hole through the center of her life.

And it was certainly before he picked up his phone and Jules told him he was out of time, and he knew (somewhere inside hadn't he always known, even if he didn't want to know?) that the only thing for him to do was to get as far away from both of them as quickly as he could. No warnings, no explanations. Just *away*.

What can he say about that now? What can he say about any of this? Anything bad anyone wants to think about what he did, he gets it.

Anything bad anyone wants to think about him, he already thinks it about himself.

~

Owen lands in Austin a little before midnight.

When he steps off the jetway, it's hot and muggy, the Texas air thick even this late at night. He takes off his leather jacket, slings it over his backpack. Then he heads toward ground transportation and the parking lot that houses the rental cars, his reservation paid for in advance, his membership to the rental car's gold club helping him avoid talking with anyone in person. Hopefully.

It's not easy renting a car with a New Zealand driver's license. It sets off alarms. He's prepared for this. He has prepared for all of this.

The computer sends him to spot 85, where a small SUV is waiting.

The First Time I Saw Him

He gets in, turns the key that is already in the ignition, and heads out of the airport parking lot and onto the familiar highway toward downtown.

Five years, ten months, and twenty-four days ago, time stopped.

He hadn't called Bailey, even when he made it to Vancouver. Even though it nearly killed him not to.

He'd forced himself to put sixty-eight hours and eight thousand miles between them before he dared to call his daughter—even on an encrypted app—to even put into the world that amount of risk.

When Bailey picked up, Owen had told her that he didn't have much time to explain. And she told him she knew about her mother, Kate. She knew about her mother and (more urgently) she knew about Kate's father, Nicholas. Bailey's grandfather, Nicholas.

Does she even remember telling Owen that? She was so upset, her tears coming through the phone, so he doesn't know. But he'll never forget.

Five years, ten months, and twenty-one days ago, Owen stood on a street corner in Wellington, New Zealand, and, from the other side of the world, he heard his daughter's tears and he heard her say the name Nicholas Bell. And a new kind of clock started.

This was the moment he started to plan.

~

Through the car windows, downtown Austin comes into view.

South Congress Avenue is busy, even after midnight—a concert letting out at the Moody Theater, people waiting for their rideshares in front of the Paramount, the patio at Lamberts still overflowing with late-night barbecue.

Owen takes a left and drives up to the condominium on Second Street—the renovated firehouse, now coveted loft apartments.

He finds a parking spot and approaches the front doors. He doesn't recognize the doorman standing there. He is new. Or, at least, newer than fifteen years.

"How can I help you?" the doorman asks him.

"Eight D."

The doorman tilts his head, takes Owen in. "Pretty late for a visitor," he says. "Is he expecting you?"

Owen hikes his backpack higher on his shoulder. He doesn't answer.

"Who should I say is here?"

"Tell him it's his son-in-law."

Somewhere Along the Line, It Becomes About the Sunrise . . .

In the morning, I play it back in my head, like a mantra.

Like a magic trick.

Owen is standing in front of me, as though it has been five minutes as opposed to more than five years. His wedding ring is still on his finger, his eyes locking into mine. And he is whispering in my ear—his lips against my cheek, his arm near my arm. Like he belonged that close. Like any other day of him belonging that close.

My husband.

I've been up for hours, sitting on the balcony off my bedroom, the light coming in from the east, soft and comforting. The light is one of my favorite things about my house—a small Craftsman two blocks from Palisades Park and the Santa Monica beaches and the Pacific Ocean.

The balcony gets the best hit of that gentle morning light. *Our favorite sunrise*, as Bailey says, surrounded by the quiet enclave of my neighborhood: five one-way streets, only local foot traffic, families who all know each other and have lived here for generations. This morning, though, none of it is offering its usual solace.

I take a sip of my coffee and go over it again. Owen standing in front of me. I circle through every detail of the brief exchange. Owen in the showroom and then, just as quickly, gone.

What was he doing before I noticed him standing there? Which direction had he come from? I feel like I saw him walk in, but had I missed it? Had he come in earlier in the day and I missed him then?

It doesn't seem possible. It doesn't seem possible that I wouldn't know that Owen was there.

I didn't mention any of it to Bailey last night—her father's brief appearance. His disappearance.

If we had been alone at dinner, I might have talked through it with her. It was good that we weren't alone, so I could process it on my own first. It was good that the new boyfriend, Shep (a little too new to be labeled boyfriend yet), walked me through his entire history over dim sum and garlic-butter noodles and heaping bowls of spicy soup.

I forced myself to focus as Shep emphasized all sorts of things in an effort to impress me (Harvard University, Bridgewater, his parents' country estate in Bedford, New York). None of that impressed me. But the way he held on to Bailey's hand and laughed genuinely at everything she said—that did.

Bailey. I consider calling her. But it's just past 8 a.m. She will be showered, pouring herself some coffee, getting ready to dive into work. I don't want to hit her with this at the beginning of her day. And I can't discuss her father with her on the phone anyway.

I take a deep breath in, the salty air centering me. But I can't shake the feeling that it wasn't just a random visit—that it wasn't just that enough time had passed, that Owen started to feel safe enough that he could come to see me. I can't shake the feeling that it's the opposite. Suddenly, it feels less safe than if he'd stayed away.

This is when my phone buzzes.

I look down at my cell to see an incoming call. I check the caller ID, the Los Angeles Lakers main office number popping up. It's a safe guess that it's the team doctor calling, wanting to make plans to get together.

Jules (forever my dearest, most indefatigable friend) became friendly with the doctor after interviewing him for a piece in the *Chronicle*—and she'd insisted on introducing us the last time she came to town for a visit.

Despite my reluctance, I understood why Jules wanted to introduce us. He is kind and smart and openhearted. I'd want to introduce him to my best friend too, if my best friend were open to being involved with anyone in a real way. Which, apparently, I'm still not.

It isn't that I'm sitting at home, sad and brooding. I'm not waiting by the window with a lamp on. I have my work, which continues to fulfill me; and I have my close friends, whom I love; and, most importantly, I have Bailey and the little family we've managed to keep strong. The family that we've managed to make strong—the days of Bailey and me failing to understand each other, far in the rearview. It's the two of us, together, first and foremost. And then it's also the family from which Bailey came—all of whom have embraced me, becoming my family too.

And still. I'm nowhere close to wanting to pick up the doctor's call. I'm not interested in meeting him for dinner or drinks or a walk by the beach.

I'm not interested in pretending I'm not (still) someone else's wife.

So I hit decline and start to put my phone back down on the small side table when a text comes through.

It's an international phone number I don't recognize. A +61 in front of it. The country code is familiar to me. I had a client who had a vacation home in Kiama, a beachside town just outside of Sydney. She'd had a +61 code.

Sydney. Australia.

I click on the text.

Check your pocket.

My breath lands in my throat and I quickly reply to the text.

Who is this?

But I get an automated reply, coming up fast and final: *The person you're trying to reach is not accepting messages.*

Check your pocket. I head inside, walking at a fast clip straight to my bedroom, and over to the closet. I pull out the dress I was wearing yesterday, reaching into the pockets. There's nothing inside either of them. What else had I been wearing? I walk into my office to find my leather motorcycle jacket draped over the small bench by my desk.

I reach into the first pocket, nothing there. And I start to feel relief. This is probably a crank, or a scam. Just a wrong number.

Then I reach into the other pocket and feel something hard and small.

A flash drive.

My heartbeat quickens, my skin heating up. My first question to myself isn't: What is this?

My first question to myself also contains the start of an answer: *Why did Owen need me to have this?*

The doorbell rings, startling me. I walk back out onto the balcony and look down over the railing's edge, down to the sidewalk below. A repairman stands at my front door, wearing a SoCalGas uniform. He is burly and large, his thick muscles pushing out over the short shirtsleeves.

I call down to him. "Can I help you?"

He squints up at me, blocks his eyes from the sun.

"Sorry to trouble you, miss. We have reports of a gas leak from your neighbors. The Waldmans?"

The Waldmans live in a Dutch Colonial two doors down from me.

The First Time I Saw Him

Two doors closer to Ocean Park and Main Street and South Santa Monica—with its surf stores and fruit stands and gourmet coffee shops. Lydia Waldman grew up in that house. Now she is raising her girls here. Twin girls, and two yellow Labs.

"Are they okay?"

"They're fine. I just need to get inside to check the line, if that's all right. Make sure it's not coming from here?"

I look up the block toward the Waldmans. I see a white pickup truck on the corner. It could be this repairman's truck, but it could also not be his. I can't make out the logo from here. I can't be sure.

As if reading my hesitation, he gives me a warm smile. "I can give you my worker ID number, if you'd like to call it in to my supervisor," he says. "Can't be too safe these days, can you?"

"No. Sure."

I head back inside, the flash drive heavy in my hand. I will call that supervisor before I let the repairman in, before I let anyone in. I'll text Lydia Waldman too.

But as I hit the staircase, my phone buzzes again. Same international number that I don't recognize. Same +61. Another text coming through.

Get out of the house. Now.

At Twenty-Two, Something's Always Broken

Bailey rips the wrapper off the fortune cookie from last night's dinner.

It's not the healthiest breakfast, that's for sure. But a quick trip to the fridge reveals that it's either the cellophane-wrapped cookie or her roommate's questionable, recently expired cherry yogurt. So the fortune cookie it is.

Bailey breaks it open, looking for the fortune inside. Sadly though, the cookie's empty. If she were a superstitious person (she's not, really) that doesn't feel like the best sign for the day ahead. But, then again, it's not as bad as those fortunes that you sometimes get that aren't a fortune at all. Like the time that Hannah got a fortune that simply read: *Believe!* Or the one that Bailey herself got the night before she started her job: *If you think something's too good to be true, it is.*

No, that was not a fortune.

It turned out, it was more like a premonition.

Bailey is the casting assistant for an acclaimed alum of her university—Alice Sleight of the famed Sleight Casting Agency. When Bailey applied for the position, Alice said she wanted to give a young graduate a great first work experience—that the hours wouldn't be too intensive, that the job would also allow time to work on outside projects.

Alice asked Bailey, during that interview, if she had a project she was working on. She told Bailey that it was (in fact) a prerequisite of her getting hired.

Bailey filled her in on the rest, excitedly. For her senior thesis, she wrote the first act of a musical (a modern retelling of Pandora's Box from Pandora's point of view), and by some miracle her professor thought it showed real promise and shared it with a theater producer in New York. The theater producer liked it so much that he asked Bailey to send him act two when she was done with it. Act three.

Alice said that she loved hearing this. That her husband was a visual artist and so she understood that passion—and what it means to be devoted to it.

Then she went on to explain that she was paring way back and only needed someone part-time. Nine-to-two. A dream learning opportunity! And one that would leave plenty of time for Bailey to focus on her own art.

Bailey didn't realize, of course, that apparently Alice meant 9 a.m. to 2 a.m. Alice calling her all hours of the day and night with emergencies.

Once, Bailey was unavailable for an eighteen-minute window (10 p.m. to 10:18 p.m.) in which Alice decided she desperately needed to reach her. Alice sent thirty-eight texts in those eighteen minutes. Firing her, then hiring her again. Then firing her again.

So it is.

Who needs sleep at twenty-two?

At least, this is what Bailey tells herself. It motivates her to spend every free moment working on her musical. (As if she needs more motivation.)

And, on the plus side, she can work from her own apartment, and she loves her apartment. It's in the heart of Venice, overlooking Abbot Kinney Boulevard, which is exactly where she and her college roommates wanted to be, now that the UCLA music program is behind them and their lives (as underfunded as three young theater

The First Time I Saw Him

kids' lives are) are sweeping out before them. They had to pick between proximity to Abbot Kinney and air-conditioning. They chose Abbot Kinney.

Bailey shoves the rest of the fortuneless fortune cookie into her mouth and heads to her keyboard—which she's set up underneath the window that's opened all the way to let the breeze in.

She pulls her hair behind her ears, takes a seat at her keyboard, and starts to get to work.

But then her phone buzzes.

She expects it to be her boss with her first frantic, pretend-emergency request of the day. But she looks down to see CHARLIE pop up on her phone screen, an incoming call from her uncle.

Bailey's Uncle Charlie. They usually talk on Friday evenings—and every Tuesday evening when her cousins are with him. But a call early on a weekday morning isn't entirely unusual. Sometimes he calls on his way to work. Sometimes he calls just to say hello. Sometimes, Bailey knows, Charlie just calls to make up for the times he couldn't.

So she is smiling when she picks up his call. She is smiling until she hears the sound of her uncle's voice—desperate and clipped—jumping in before she even has a chance to say hello to him.

"Are you with Hannah?" he asks.

"What?"

"Is Hannah with you?"

"No. Is she supposed to be? It's eight in the morning."

"Bailey, is Justin out front?"

Justin is the bodyguard her grandfather hired to keep eyes on Bailey. The same way Charlie's twins, Bailey's cousins, have bodyguards to watch over them.

Bailey looks out the window. On a workday, she can often make out Justin's Jeep diagonally across the street, near the sunglass store. Near the fruit stand with the fresh watermelon juice.

But sometimes Justin is somewhere else entirely. This morning he must be somewhere else.

She scans her corner of Abbott Kinney, unable to spot him at first glance. It is starting to get busier with early morning traffic, folks lining up at the coffee shop downstairs, two SoCalGas repairmen standing by her building's front door.

"I don't see him."

"You don't see him?" Charlie sounds frantic. He isn't trying to hide it. "Shouldn't he be there?"

"He probably is. Charlie, you're freaking me out. What's going on?"

"You need to get to Hannah and you need to go."

"Go where?"

"Call me back when you are somewhere safe and I'll fill you in."

"Is it Nicholas?"

She doesn't refer to Nicholas as Grandpa, not all the time. At that moment, for some reason, it's Nicholas. Nicholas who was diagnosed with heart failure last year. He'd had a pacemaker put in to buy him more time. He'd been fine at Easter. He'd been fine when he flew out for her birthday. He was *just fine*, he promised Bailey, again and again.

But Bailey would put her hand on his heart, to feel the beating, like a certain kind of proof. Now she held her hand on her own heart, waiting for Charlie's answer.

"Charlie, is this about Nicholas? Is he okay?"

"Nothing's okay," Charlie says.

And Bailey starts to move.

You Can't Go Home and You Can't Stay Here

I clutch the flash drive in my hand, turning quickly.

My staircase is visible from the windows by the front door, so there's no going out that way. There's no going out from any of the first-floor exits and not running into the man (whoever he is) pretending there's a gas leak, pretending in that SoCalGas uniform.

Instead, I race back to my bedroom and grab the backpack from under the bed, putting the flash drive in my front pocket. I take the ladder up to the attic and pop open the back window. There is a trellis crawling down the back of the house, into the soft landing of my small backyard. This is why I chose this house. This trellis.

I climb down it, the easy ladder-rungs, and drop to the grass.

I race to the back gate and let myself out into the small alleyway that separates me from the Blauners' house. I close the gate behind myself, locking it—when a loud crack startles me. Is it coming from inside my house? A window breaking? My bay window? The front door being kicked in?

Is it unrelated?

I'm not waiting to find out.

I move quickly, unlocking the Blauners' back door, heading into their small backyard. If they are sitting at the table in their sunroom and see me through their windows, they will be confused, but not too confused. They certainly won't be scared.

I have a key, so I can get their mail when they are away. I give them their mail and they give me a way out.

I walk through the backyard, keeping my head down. I don't look up as I pass by their kitchen window or their living room doors. I don't look up until I am in their front yard and out their front gate, walking quickly down Fraser, toward the ocean, toward Barnard Way. My backpack tight on my back.

When I get to Barnard Way—the ocean just beyond it, the ocean and the beach—I start to run.

I run past Hart Avenue and Wadsworth, and circle down toward the beach, early morning joggers and dogwalkers and pedestrians dotting the way. Most don't seem to care or notice that I'm running so fast—though a few do a double take. A few turn and watch as I pick up speed.

I ignore them. I ignore everything until I get to the small hotel by the water, Shutters on the Beach, a bevy of taxis always out front. It's a lovely hotel—plush and storied, but unobtrusive—that looks like it belongs in Martha's Vineyard as opposed to so close to the Santa Monica Pier with its Ferris wheel, its gritty boardwalk.

I slow my gait and nod at the doormen as I hop into the first taxi in line and tell the driver where I'm going.

I ask him to take Appian Way, for as long as it will let him take it, to get to the closest ramp down to the PCH. I ask him to avoid Ocean Avenue and Main Street.

Then I text Bailey, *Late drink?*

And I turn around, look out the back window. No white pickup truck, SoCalGas logo or not.

I have a paper clip in my backpack. I pull it out and dislodge the SIM card, pull it free from my phone.

The First Time I Saw Him

I open the window. And I throw the SIM card out onto the street. Some car, perhaps one of the taxis with their engines purring behind us, will soon run it over. I won't be there to see it happen.

I shut the window and turn back to the driver.

"Please go," I say. "We need to move now."

Bailey's Gonna Get There

You always have a moment to take three breaths.

This was the first thing that Hannah told her. When she started preparing Bailey for this moment, this moment they hoped wouldn't be happening, Hannah said to make sure that Bailey stopped and took three breaths. *You have time*, she said. Inhale for four, hold it, exhale for eight.

If you do this first, Hannah said, *everything you have to do next will be easier.*

They had, in fact, done run-throughs to get ready for this. Bailey didn't even fight Hannah on the run-throughs because there was no fighting Hannah on this. On being prepared, on doing things that would keep Bailey safe.

Something happens when you have a mother who never asks you what to do. Who instead has the answers for you. You believe her that she knows.

This is probably why it's almost as if Hannah is standing in front of Bailey now, reminding her why she's ready for this, reminding her exactly how to get herself where she needs to go: Bailey lives in a secure building. And Justin is somewhere outside, even if Bailey doesn't know where exactly outside.

Justin is good at staying close while keeping his distance. If Bailey is going somewhere at night—a restaurant with friends, or a bar—he stays in his car outside. In case, quickly, she needs him.

That is the first thing she is supposed to do, call Justin. The second is to not wait when he doesn't answer.

Bailey looks down at Hannah's text. *Late drink?*

This is what they'd arranged for Hannah to text, at any time of day or night, so Bailey knows the status quo has changed.

Bailey is already moving when the text comes in. She's been moving since Charlie's phone call. She has been trying not to ask herself: What changed? Her first thought, her biggest fear: Does it involve her father? And what did Charlie not want to say about Nicholas? What was Charlie not willing to say about him over the phone?

Nothing's okay.

Bailey fills the kitchen sink with soapy water, drops her cell phone inside. Then she heads to her front door, leaving the apartment empty-handed. She is empty-handed except for what she grabs from the stack of keys on the wall by the front door. Two keys, each one on its own key chain: one blue and one red, both of which she pops in her back pocket, heading into the hallway.

She walks past the elevator and moves quickly to the fire exit and the staircase beyond the door. She hurries down the two flights to the super's apartment. Her building's super.

When she gets to his door, she knocks several times in quick succession.

"Hello?" she says. "It's Bailey Michaels."

There is no answer, which makes it easier. She pulls the blue key from her back pocket and lets herself in.

For an extra two hundred dollars a month, the super has allowed for this arrangement that Hannah has made with him. He has allowed for Bailey to have access to his apartment for the sole reason that once (only once) she might need to walk through his apartment

The First Time I Saw Him

to use his private exit. His separate exit. The only exit in the building that isn't attached to the lobby and the front door.

The exit that leads into the building next door, which the super also manages. It takes you to a different lobby—unseen by anyone who is watching from the street, who may be focused on Bailey's lobby door.

Now, Bailey walks out of the apartment and into the adjacent lobby, and the elevator banks that take her down to parking level four.

She has a car waiting here. This isn't the car she uses every day. This is a different car, a small Jetta that Hannah's best friend, Jules, purchased and registered under her name. Not Hannah's. Not Bailey's.

She pulls the red key from her back pocket and unlocks the Jetta, remembering Hannah's instructions. There is a full tank of gas. And there's a full trunk. *Don't open the trunk. Get in the car and move.*

Bailey reverses out of the garage quickly, using the exit that takes her out to Venice Boulevard, around the corner from her own garage entrance. Where they (whoever they are, wherever they are) won't think to be looking.

She turns left and then left again until she is heading in the direction of the Pacific Coast Highway and Hannah.

Only then, and only for a moment, does she let herself cry.

Malibu Road Is Private for a Reason

On the highway, the taxi passes the exit for Entrada Drive and my workshop.

Despite my heart racing, despite the fact I know it's not possible, I feel a pull to ask the driver to turn that way, to get to pretend (for a little longer) this is any other day. To spend it at my workshop in Rustic Canyon, a beautiful slice of Los Angeles right off the Pacific Coast Highway—hilly and quiet and incredibly private.

My workshop is on a small road that dead-ends into a cul-de-sac. It's in a ranch-style house with hedges out front and a large side yard. It has plenty of room for my lathe, my oversize bookshelves filled with wood blanks, and for the sizable storage shed that houses my larger pieces in various stages of production.

There are only a handful of other houses on the road, which is across the street from a Eucalyptus Garden, the backyard offering foggy views of the ocean and the mountains and Malibu out in the distance.

I open the window as we pass the exit, my workshop hidden by that beautiful canyon. But I stay quiet, and the driver keeps going, not taking the exit, heading past Topanga Canyon and toward Malibu. Toward Malibu, and toward my destination: a beachfront house on the end of Malibu Road.

It's a house that belongs to one of my clients—a client who is now married to my former fiancé, Jake.

The client is an actress who I started working with shortly after

I moved to Los Angeles, building furniture for nearly every room of her Malibu beach house. She is bright and sarcastic and beautiful—and I had a feeling, as soon as I met her, that she and Jake might like each other. I had such a strong feeling that, even though I wasn't in the business of setting up my former fiancé, I felt compelled to introduce them. And I'm so glad that I did. They fell in love and got married and are expecting their first child together. Jake now the best version of Jake there seems to be.

They spend most of their time in New York City, but they kept this house on Malibu Road, Jake's name not on the deed.

That part—not putting Jake on the deed—they did for me. For me and for Bailey. So no one would think to look for us there. At least not quickly.

I ask the taxi to let me off half a mile away from their house, at the Malibu Country Mart—a large outdoor shopping area dotted with fancy stores and bakeries and restaurants, a sign announcing that paparazzi aren't welcome. The surfers and the beautiful locals are all more interesting to look at than I am, which makes disappearing here feel possible.

I pay the driver in cash and slide into the local coffee shop in case he is watching where I go. In case he, or anyone, figures out that it was me who he dropped here.

The coffee shop is already bustling inside and on the back patio, Malibu locals taking in the early morning sun and heat from the comfort of their cappuccinos. Their oversize green juices.

I head out a different exit without ordering anything and jog toward the northern edge of the Country Mart—and the crosswalk that runs across the highway. Toward a small residential neighborhood on the other side, the beach and ocean just beyond it.

As soon as the light turns, I race across the highway and past

The First Time I Saw Him

Ralph's supermarket and the animal hospital and the gas station. I jog through a parking lot that lets me out on the private (and quiet) of Malibu Road, Jake's house in the distance.

The house is a stunner: all glass and beach views, my rustic wood furniture visible through the filmy windows, the large steel doors.

I don't enter through the front doors though. I have a remote to the garage in my bag. Bailey has the other one. I let myself in, closing the garage quickly behind me.

I head into the house, passing through the small mudroom, and into the large great room—a living room and a home office and a kitchen all wrapped into one.

I turn on the lights in the kitchen and the television in the living room, finding CNN on the remote, as I pull a new burner phone out of my bag.

Then I tap in Grady's cell phone number, as opposed to calling him at the US Marshals office, an extra layer of protection, even though Grady Bradford is the one US marshal Owen trusted. The one who, over time, I've come to trust too. There's no trusting anyone completely, though—not at this moment.

Grady picks up on the first ring, like he's been waiting. Because he has.

"Is Owen okay?" I ask.

"Where are you, Hannah?"

"You first, Grady."

I'm turning up the volume on the television, moving through the house quickly and closing the electric blinds.

I'm focused on that, on closing the blinds, and on what I think Grady is going to say, when I get my answer—or I get part of my answer—coming from the television news reporter. Nicholas Bell, infamous criminal defense lawyer, has died.

I think I must have heard wrong, my back to the television screen.

But I turn quickly, and there it is, Nicholas's face on the news. A slightly younger Nicholas dressed in a suit, standing outside court, microphones bouncing up against his face. The chyron parroting the news anchor, screaming the finality, the words in bold on the bottom of the screen.

NICHOLAS BELL, LAWYER FOR THE ORGANIZATION CRIME SYNDICATE, PRONOUNCED DEAD AT TEXAS HILL COUNTRY HOME

"Holy shit," I say.

My breath leaves my chest, my eyes drilling into the screen.

"Nicholas is dead?"

"He is," he says. "I'm sorry to be the one to tell you that. He died in his sleep early this morning."

My questions start to come out hot and quick. "How, Grady? What happened?"

"He was out at the lake. They think it was a heart attack. But I'm going to head out to the lake this afternoon, try to get the details in person. It's a real tiny office out there, obviously. Just the coroner, not even an assistant, at least not one who I can reach. Can't get any real information on the phone."

I try to center myself, tears filling my eyes. A tightness pressing in hard on my ribs.

Nicholas is gone. Nicholas who, over these last five years, has evolved from someone that I feared to a person that I deeply trust. The person who I've come to trust most, at least when it comes to Bailey.

How can I begin to explain that evolution between us? Despite all

The First Time I Saw Him

the ways I initially bucked against it, it was impossible for me not to move toward Nicholas. It was impossible, on the simplest level, because of how Nicholas was—and the kindness he showed, over and over again, to Bailey.

It wasn't just that Nicholas showed up for Bailey for the proud-grandparent highlight reel—for her prom pictures and graduation and her musical opening nights. It was that Nicholas wanted (more than anything) to be there for the rest of it. The good things and the hard things too. Nicholas insisted on being there for everything. When Bailey got a concussion on her senior high school class trip to the Arches in Moab, Nicholas got on a plane as fast as I did, walking into that small Utah hospital within minutes of me. I remember the feel of his hand on my shoulder as I turned around to find him there, one of many reminders that I wasn't in it alone.

When Bailey was doing the intensive summer training institute at the Williamstown Theatre Festival, her house was ransacked and robbed. That time, Nicholas beat me to Massachusetts, providing a safe haven for Bailey and her roommates at a local hotel. He offered me that same small squeeze of my shoulder when I walked into the hotel room, a silent acknowledgment that he intended to be someone I could count on.

Again and again, Nicholas proved that when it came to the person who mattered more to me than anything in the world, I had someone to help hold her.

Which is why, over time, he became my first phone call when anything went wrong with Bailey. When things went right with her too. Nicholas earned that with his commitment to her. He earned Bailey's desire to spend holidays together and birthdays and college vacations. And, in the process, he earned the same thing from me.

After all, the easiest path to loving someone is when you share the most important thing together. Bailey was our most important thing. And Nicholas loved her in the same unmitigated, unapologetic way that I did. He loved her in the way that only your family can. Over time, it felt like he and I started to love each other that way too.

And now, like that, he's gone.

The heat rises up, a seizing taking hold in my chest, in my lungs. The impossible and permanent truth.

I'm suddenly without him.

"This isn't good, Hannah," Grady says. "Everything has changed."

"What does that mean?"

"The organization isn't honoring the deal you two made. You and Nicholas. That you and Bailey would be safe."

"Not honoring it how?"

"You need to let me bring you in," he says.

"Answer the question first."

"Their mandate has apparently shifted, now that Nicholas is gone. The organization wants Owen . . . however they need to get to him. You're the only known line to him. You and Bailey . . ."

I hear the rest of it before Grady even says it, my heartbeat picking up. Eighteen years haven't thawed the organization's anger toward Owen. I know as much. I know all the time in the world won't thaw what they view as Owen's betrayal (of them, of Nicholas) for turning state's evidence and testifying against them.

But Bailey and I are immune to that vendetta. Or we are supposed to be. Except now, apparently, the agreement Nicholas made with his former clients to keep Bailey and me safe isn't being honored—now that Nicholas isn't here to make sure his clients honor it.

It confuses me, all the same. Any decision like this—any large shift—would have to be approved by the head of the organization,

The First Time I Saw Him

wouldn't it? It wouldn't just need to be approved by him, but also ordered by him.

Francis Campano Pointe II, or Frank, as Nicholas referred to him, has run the organization for decades (his father before that, his maternal grandfather before his father). Frank brought Nicholas into the organization in the first place. He was Nicholas's most important client for most of his career. And the person—most importantly—with whom Nicholas arranged to secure Bailey's and my safety.

Didn't Nicholas believe that we could count on Frank to keep his word? Didn't Nicholas say they were like family to each other? Why, even in Nicholas's absence, would that shift so dramatically? And so quickly?

Get out of the house. Now.

"Mom..."

I turn to see Bailey walking into the living room. She is in a tank top and ripped jeans, her long hair still wet from the shower, her eyes red and bright from crying. I wonder what she knows about her grandfather already, about what is happening. What has she learned in the last hour since her life started to unravel all around her?

My eyes dart to the television screen. Her grandfather's face is no longer splashed across the screen, thankfully, but the chyron is still going, the words still ticking by for her to read. In whole, in part.

NICHOLAS BELL, LAWYER FOR THE ORGANIZATION CRIME SYNDICATE, PRONOUNCED DEAD AT TEXAS HILL COUNTRY HOME

"Grady, I'm going to call you back."

"No, you need to listen to me first, okay? The doorman at

Nicholas's condo in the city says that someone who identified himself as Nicholas's son-in-law came to see Nicholas late last night."

"What are you talking about?"

"The doorman didn't let him in, but I've got two guys watching down the security tapes. I'm trying to confirm if it was really Owen. And if it was, we have a real problem here unless I can stop it from breaking. Because if it breaks, people are going to connect the dots to suggest Owen may have had something to do with Nicholas's death."

I take that in, trying to make sense of it. Could it have been Owen at Nicholas's condo? Why would Owen have gone from the showroom in Los Angeles to downtown Austin to see Nicholas? But I don't offer that question out loud. I don't say anything that suggests I know where Owen was last night.

I'm looking at Bailey, Bailey who is looking back at me. Bailey who is about to find out that her grandfather is lost to her.

"But I thought . . . didn't you just say that Nicholas was found out at the lake? At The Sanctuary?"

"That doesn't matter. What matters is this is the first legitimate claim of someone spotting Owen in five years. And Nicholas is found dead that night? In the same city? Does that sound like a coincidence?"

The flash drive grows heavier in my pocket. Owen's skin and eyes and hands last night so close to my skin.

Bailey is looking more and more scared. Her eyes are wild, goose bumps covering her skin. It probably isn't helping that my face is giving away that I feel the same.

Which is when I let myself know what I don't want to know.

This is why Owen showed up last night.

This is why I got those texts this morning.

It was Owen warning me about what he had to do, or what he was still doing. Even if I don't know why he's doing it just yet.

The First Time I Saw Him

That's the job now. To start to figure out the why.

I hold Bailey's gaze, wiping the fear off my face. Behind her the news report has switched again. Nicholas is back on the screen. I look between her face and his, the similarity too close to be comfortable.

And I'm already starting to piece together what I need to know. Why the grief of Nicholas's loss feels riddled with something else—something urgent and incoming—that I need to understand. Something I feel certain that Nicholas would want me to understand, if he were still here to tell me.

But Bailey starts to turn around. She starts to turn around and see for herself that her grandfather is gone. I need to tell her first—not just about her grandfather, but also about her father. About what needs to happen now.

"Hannah," Grady says. "Are you listening to me?"

No, I'm not. I'm only listening to myself. I'm only paying attention to what I know I need to do now.

"Not anymore," I say.

This is when I hang up.

~

"So Dad was there last night?" Bailey asks. "At the design center?"

We're standing in Jake's garage, the trunk to the Jetta open. There are several large suitcases and duffel bags inside—clothes I packed for Bailey, clothes for me, and, hidden beneath them, a gray computer case, which I pull out now.

I nod. "He was."

"How could you not tell me?"

I unzip the computer case, trying to figure out how to answer Bailey—and answer her quickly. It is a fine line, figuring out how to tell Bailey what she needs to know while not entirely overwhelming her.

Bailey, who is shaking before me. Her face red, her eyes averting mine. Overwhelmed and angry and shocked.

More than anything, I'm registering her shock. Her grandfather is gone, which I see her struggling to even begin to process. Her father is—inexplicably—back.

I have five minutes to calm her down before we need to be on the road. I have less than five minutes to calm her down and to open this flash drive. To study it. To do both of those things and to do them well.

Then I need us to be out of here, whether she is ready for that or not.

I need to be on the road, moving somewhere away from here.

"I couldn't exactly talk to you about all of this in front of someone else, Bails," I say. "And I needed a little time to process first. I needed to first try and figure out what he was doing there."

"What did you come up with?" she asks.

"I'm still working on it."

I slam the trunk shut and pull the laptop out of its case, resting it on the car. This clean laptop that has never been connected to the internet. That has had its wireless capability disabled. This laptop that will be untraceable—the laptop and any information from the flash drive that I download onto it. Available to no one. But us.

The computer powers on. I plug the flash drive into the laptop, the two of us standing side by side as I click on the drive and a screen pops up.

The home page takes on a circle formation, a circle formation with arrows and edges. A marine compass.

The First Time I Saw Him

"What the hell is that?" Bailey says. "Is that a compass or something?"

"A marine compass," I say. "Yes."

I shake my head, unsure why Owen has put this compass on here. It gives me pause though. It makes me wonder for a moment if Owen knows—how could he know?—my plan for how to get Bailey out of here. The plan I haven't even told her yet. That I've said, aloud, to no one.

I lean in closer to the screen and click on the one folder in the corner—a folder labeled PHOTO ALBUMS. Several files pop open. Five photo albums in total. Owen has named each of them. *Sausalito; O & H Honeymoon; Baby Bailey; Family; Hannah's Work.*

No directions. No obvious message.

"What are we supposed to do with this?" Bailey asks.

I shake my head. I don't know.

"Are they ordered somehow?"

"They don't seem to be," I say. "But that's a good question . . ."

I open the finder and select date modified.

And I click on the album Owen created first. The photo album that he labeled *Sausalito*.

The album has several photographs in it. Some of them are of our floating home and the docks, some of young Bailey and Owen racing down those docks, some are of Owen's closest friend, Carl, and his wife, Patty. Carl and Patty who—despite their long friendship with Owen, or maybe because of it—weren't exactly kind to me after Owen disappeared.

Several of the photographs seem to include Carl and Patty, which seems odd. One of the photographs even includes Carl and his brother, Daniel. Owen standing between them, the three of them laughing.

"Why would he want us to have all these photos of Carl and Patty?" Bailey asks, confused.

"I was wondering the same," I say.

I zero in on the photograph of Owen with Carl and Daniel. I zero in on Owen's face, and I know there is a reason. If there are photographs of Carl and his family, there is of course a reason he is sharing them with me.

Because Owen isn't just giving me photographs. Owen is giving me messages. Private messages that only I can decipher. Just in case the flash drive gets intercepted. Just in case it gets into hands that aren't mine. I take another glance at the last photograph—the one with Carl's brother. Carl's arm wrapped lovingly around Owen's shoulder.

Then I look at the clock on the top of the laptop. The time is ticking down, ticking down in a way that's making me anxious.

Two minutes. We have two minutes before we should be out of here. Two minutes before I need to start getting us to where we are going next—before we start putting distance between us and our last known address. Our last known city. And the people who are looking for us here. They'll be looking for us everywhere we have ever been. My studio, Bailey's boss's office. Our friends' houses. They'll crawl the airports—LAX and Burbank and Long Beach. All public transportation hubs. Anywhere that gives us an easy exit to somewhere else.

Owen's text races to the forefront of my mind: *Get out of the house.*

I slam the laptop shut.

"We're out of time," I say. "We've got to go."

"What about the photographs? Shouldn't we keep going through them?"

The First Time I Saw Him

"That's why you're driving," I say. "I'll do it on the way. I have a lot of things to do on the way."

"On the way to where?" Bailey calls out.

I open the passenger-side door, start to get in.

"Anywhere but here."

The 101 Is Never Pretty

One of the first things I did when I moved to Los Angeles—and set up my new studio—was put in cameras.

I installed security cameras at Bailey's apartment and my Santa Monica home and throughout my work studio: monitoring the perimeter of the properties, especially surrounding my studio.

While Bailey drives, I open my backpack. I pull out a new burner phone and a new tablet. I power up the tablet and the sole application, which links to the camera feeds.

I pull up all fifteen feeds—the videos of all three properties springing to life.

Bailey's apartment is quiet, empty. That is the least surprising. The security measures to even get into the building (locked keypad, day doorman, live-in super) make it harder to organically infiltrate. My house is empty too. No one milling around.

But my work studio is a different story. There are two men walking around in the backyard. One of them is peering into the back window.

Both of them are in SoCalGas uniforms. The guy peering in the window looks a little like the guy who was at my door earlier this morning, but I'm not sure.

I zoom in and take screenshots of their faces, screenshots of their movement.

Then I forward the photographs to my only neighbor in that

small, isolated cul-de-sac. I forward her the photographs with nothing written in the text.

My neighbor knows what to do if she ever gets photographs of my property from a number she doesn't recognize. She knows to call the police and tell them that people are trespassing. She knows to lock her doors.

"So are you going to say it or not?" Bailey asks.

I turn and look at her, the Pacific Coast Highway floating by outside the driver-side window, the ocean in the distance, the late-morning traffic going mostly toward Los Angeles as opposed to farther away.

"Say what?"

"Dad shows up on the same night that Grandpa dies?" she says. "That's so fucking weird."

"I know," I say. "It's weird. I won't try to convince you that it isn't."

"That doesn't make me feel any better, Mom."

Bailey purses her lips, starts nervously biting her nails. Her eyes wide with sadness. It squeezes something deep inside me, how much it makes her look like the younger version of herself—the guarded, unapproachable teenager who wanted nothing to do with me, who I could never seem to do right by.

It took me a long time to understand that Bailey wasn't being snarky or difficult, back then. (How easy and wrongheaded to name her fears in that way.) Bailey had just been scared—for different reasons than she is scared now—but scared all the same. She'd been scared to trust anyone who wasn't her father, especially someone coming in as hot as I did. She'd been scared that she didn't even know how to trust someone who wasn't her father. We'd had that in common.

The First Time I Saw Him

I reach over and gently move Bailey's hand away from her mouth, give it a squeeze, grateful for how far we've come since then. Grateful that, even though I fail at times, I'm now much better at knowing how to ease her.

"Bails," I say. "This is all a lot to process, for me too. But, for what it's worth, I am certain that Owen had nothing to do with Nicholas's death. Grady didn't give me any indications that foul play was involved. And your grandpa has had a serious heart condition for a while now. You know that. And you know your father. You know that he would never hurt your grandfather."

I say it emphatically. Because I know that's what she needs to hear—and I know that it's true. Owen wouldn't hurt Nicholas. He's not built that way.

Bailey takes that in, and I can see her start to relax, the fear dropping out of her eyes.

"Yeah . . . I guess that's true."

I nod. "Good."

"But how do you explain it then?" she asks. "You know, all of this happening at the same time?"

"If I'm being honest? I'm still figuring that out . . ."

She nods. And I leave out the other part. The part I do know, the part left unspoken between us. That even if Owen didn't have anything to do with Nicholas's death, it's connected. Losing Nicholas, Owen coming back. It's all connected.

Get out of the house. Now.

"Where are we going anyway?" Bailey asks.

"North," I say.

"Care to be more specific?"

"Well, right now, we just need to get some distance between us and the places where they have been tracking us."

"They've been tracking us?"

I don't answer her. She knows that answer.

"How much distance?" she asks.

I have two answers for her, and they both start the same way. They start with us avoiding the major highways (no 101 or I-5, except when absolutely necessary) and taking surface roads whenever possible. We are avoiding tolls and cameras. We are going to hug the coast and take side streets and avoid any surveillance that we can.

Without the flash drive, this trip north would take us to Santa Cruz, a beachside town situated on the northern edge of Monterey Bay—home to the Mission Santa Cruz and surf shops, and (most importantly) UC Santa Cruz, where Jules spent a year teaching. And where she has a wealthy friend from graduate school who owns a boat. A forty-foot boat that is the same make and model of a yacht in Marina del Rey that over the last five years (over weekends and workdays) I learned how to operate.

A French-manufactured forty-foot boat that I studied intensively: learning how to handle the lines and operate the engines and work the thrusters. Spending my weekends navigating to Catalina Island and the Channel Islands and San Diego. First, with my very patient instructor. Then, eventually, on my own.

If we follow my original plan, we will stop for the night in the hills above Scotts Valley at the house of Jules's friend, in the upland slope of the Santa Cruz Mountains, and not too far from the marina.

As soon as there is sunrise, we will drive the last eight miles to the marina and get on that forty-foot boat—and we'll pull up anchor and head to the Sea of Cortez. We'll swim in that sea and get too much sun and talk about Nicholas. We'll process that loss. We'll process the stress of all of this. And, most importantly, I'll keep Bailey safe until we navigate a way to permanently keep Bailey safe.

The First Time I Saw Him

The flash drive changes things. I just need to find out how much.

I reach for the laptop, pulling it onto my lap. The marine compass staring at me when I click open the screen.

I tap on the album Owen created most recently, the album labeled *Hannah's Work*. There are several photographs of my furniture and larger pieces, a selfie that Owen took of the two of us at one of the first exhibitions of mine that he ever went to, in Los Alamos—a small town north of Santa Barbara.

That photo of the first exhibition, bringing me back to the last exhibition.

Last night's exhibition.

What Owen said to me there. *The could have been boys still love you.* This morning's text. *Get out of the house.*

All of it is obscure. Why is he being so obscure? I know the answer is wrapped up in keeping us safe. And, maybe, keeping himself safe too.

Which is when I start to wonder how those two things are tied together now.

I click *Hannah's Work* shut and turn back to the *Sausalito* photo album, the first album he created, like a small clue of where to look first. Where to focus most.

All those photographs on our docks, with Carl and his family, Bailey's astute question about them. Why all those photos?

I power up the new phone. I have no numbers saved in there. The only numbers I need, I have long ago learned by heart.

And I call the first number I've memorized.

Patty. Carl's wife. She curates an art gallery in downtown Sausalito. I don't call Carl directly. That feels too risky. That feels like a call that someone could be watching for at this point. So it's Patty I call. Patty at her work.

"The Sausalito Collective," she answers. "This is Patty."

"Hi, it's me," I say. As though it has been five minutes, not five years.

She doesn't say anything. But she doesn't hang up. Which lets me know she may have been waiting for this call.

"I think I need to speak to your husband," I say.

"No, you don't," she says. "This has nothing to do with Carl."

I start to get off the phone. I start to let it go.

"Daniel is who you want."

"Daniel?"

It takes me a moment. Daniel is Carl's brother. Daniel who is in the photograph with Owen and Carl.

What do I know about Daniel? He lives in Morro Bay with his partner and their dogs. A beautiful house on the beach that they renovated themselves, all glass and steel. They have no kids, but a bunch of dogs, in part because of Daniel's work schedule. Which is when I remember the rest, my heart starting to race.

Daniel is a pilot.

"Give me ninety minutes," she says. "But you should head north."

"I already am," I say.

"Keep going," she says.

Then she hangs up.

~

We pull over to get gas.

While the tank fills up, we head into the convenience store to get some food. A cable news station is playing on the convenience store television. The small television over the checkout counter.

I am already thinking of Charlie, which makes it feel like I've conjured him up, because when we go to pay, the main story has shifted to Nicholas again.

The First Time I Saw Him

And it's Charlie who is staring back at me on the television screen. Charlie and his twins, hustling into their car, Charlie trying to shield them from the cameras and the microphones.

I can feel Bailey's anxiety kicking back up—her eyes glued to the screen despite knowing she should look away. I can't look away either, not when I see their faces, so scared and upset. The cameras making it all worse.

This shouldn't be surprising to me—the sheer amount of coverage. The media (especially cable media) will take any opportunity to talk about the history of organized crime, particularly a crime family as storied as the organization.

You don't have to be a media expert to see why—to see how it increases their ratings to lean into true crime, people unable to look away from anything that plays into our collective fear and fascination with organized crime and drugs and sex. Our collective fear of bad men doing bad things.

"Is that all?"

I pull my eyes from the television and look over at the young cashier, who is tabulating our variety of potato chips and nuts and drinks, a six-pack of cold brew coffees. He rings in the total.

I nod and hand him two fifty-dollar bills.

"I need to use your restroom," I say. "And that extra fifty is for you if I can use your phone for thirty seconds."

He hands over his phone and I text another number that I know by heart. Charlie's number.

Charlie, who I'm sure is worried about Bailey. Who, in the wake of losing his father, needs to know she is okay.

But, even from a random phone, it feels a little close to be reaching out to him. At the moment, it all feels so close. Which is why, just in case someone is watching his phone, I'm careful. I don't say anything about Nicholas. I don't ask how he is holding up—even though I know he is shattered too.

I keep the text simple. And I lie.

B and I are fine. heading to a friend's place in Jackson Hole. Will call you from there . . .

Then I send another text—this time to Jules. The text I most need to send.

You interested in a vacation?

This is all I'm supposed to say, so she knows we're headed to Santa Cruz. So she knows we're headed to the boat.

As soon as the texts are marked delivered, I erase them from the young cashier's phone history. Then I make sure the numbers don't appear in his text history and hand his cell back to him.

He looks at me, confused. "You didn't even call anyone," he says.

"Is that your way of offering me a refund?" I ask.

In response, he pockets the fifty.

Then he points to the bathroom. "Don't use the first stall," he says. "It's always a mistake."

~

I drive.

I try Patty at exactly the ninety-minute mark, and she doesn't pick up.

We are passing through Cambria, a small seaside village, beautiful forests on one side of the road, the ocean on the other.

Reception is somewhat spotty. So I click off and try her again.

When she doesn't answer the second time, I try not to panic.

I keep my eyes on the road. I keep my eyes on the road and I keep my focus on Bailey, who sits in the passenger seat next to me, eating

The First Time I Saw Him

her snacks from the convenience store. She is on her second cold brew coffee, a large bag of jalapeño potato chips. She is downing the potato chips three at a time, trying to calm her nerves.

"What are you thinking about over there?" I ask her.

"We just passed a sign for San Francisco. Two hundred and fifty miles." She pauses. "That's not where we are headed, is it?"

I hear the rest of her question. San Francisco is close to Sausalito. San Francisco is too close to where she came from. Isn't that another place the organization would think to look for us? Another place that is categorically unsafe?

I turn and look at her. I don't want to scare her by saying the whole truth. Because even if a part of her knows it, it's scarier to hear the words coming from me. That, at the moment, nowhere is safe.

"Bails, we're not going home," I say. "We're not going near there."

She nods, relieved. Then she gets quiet. She gets quiet before she asks what she asks next.

"How did he look?" she asks.

"Your dad?"

She nods. "I mean . . . did he look like himself?"

I shake my head, thinking of how to answer her about Owen—the buzz cut hair, the sleeve of tattoos, the shape of his nose. All that wasn't familiar. But his eyes—what was behind those eyes—staring back me, entirely familiar. How do I answer most honestly? Owen looked exactly like himself. And also entirely different.

"It was all pretty quick . . ." I say.

She puts the potato chips down, wiping the grease on the side of her jeans.

"Can I tell you something crazy?" she says.

"Of course."

"I keep thinking that Dad walked past me. I swear to you, I

thought I saw him at the design center, you know? I turned and did a double take when I saw this guy. There was something about him. Like . . . the way he carried himself. It was like instinct, you know? How quickly I turned to see if it was him. I don't know if I'm just making that up now. I don't know, but it's like I felt him there, if that makes sense . . ."

"It does."

"But maybe it wasn't him. I mean, I feel like I see him all the time. So that's not new . . ." She pauses. "I just feel so upset about Grandpa, you know? Every time I think about him, I feel more upset."

I feel that in my chest, a rising up of everything Bailey has endured. That she continues to endure: the disappearance of her father, now her grandfather taken from her too.

"Me too, Bails . . ."

"And I can only say this to you, but . . . I also feel a little relieved, if that makes any sense. I feel relieved that it's not Dad. Because when I walked into Jake's house and first saw your face . . ."

"You thought something happened to your father?"

"Yeah."

I get that part also, probably better than anyone else could. The devastation and the sadness at the loss of Nicholas cuts through me. It cuts through me at the same time something else lives just beneath it. A relief. Is it fair to call it relief? Because my greatest fear when I heard Grady's voice was that he was going to tell me that something terrible had happened to Owen. Owen who reappeared out of nowhere last night. His text this morning, the flash drive still heavy in my pocket.

My first terrible fear was that someone had gotten to Owen. Shortly after Owen had gotten to me.

"You weren't ready for that . . ." I say. "Neither of us was."

The First Time I Saw Him

"Yeah."

She looks back toward the passenger-side window. And I can see her trying to process it. The death that had been hovering over us since Nicholas became unwell. The death we have been trying to ready ourselves for—as if you can ever ready yourself for that kind of leveling, for that kind of grief.

Bailey rolls down the window, letting in the air and the ocean and the noise of all the passing cars. It's so loud that I almost don't hear her. I almost don't hear the question she doesn't want to ask next.

"Do we run now? Like forever?"

I think of where we were twenty-four hours ago: before Owen showed up at the design center, before the loss of Nicholas. I'd spent the afternoon participating in the First Look exhibition—making reservations to take my favorite girl (and her new friend Shep) out to get her favorite dim sum.

I think of how twenty-four hours ago this would have been the last place either of us thought we'd be.

"I think if we are learning anything," I say, "it's that nothing is forever."

In Big Sur, the Landscape Changes

We are driving through Big Sur when Patty finally picks up.

"Sorry," she says. "There was someone in the gallery. A tourist who wouldn't leave. I couldn't take a chance."

"That's okay."

"Where are you now?"

I keep my eyes on the road, the almost impossible stretch of Highway 1 laying out before me. One of my favorite roads in the world, carved into the steep divide of mountain white rock and the sea below—Bixby Canyon Bridge not too far in the distance.

Now I'm just trying to get over it, as fast as possible.

"About a hundred miles from San Jose," I say.

That's not accurate, exactly. I don't offer up where we are. I try to say where we are going. Just in case. Everything now is just in case.

"That works," she says. "Do you have somewhere to stay tonight?"

"We're set on that."

"Good. That's good. Then tomorrow morning, you need to be at the Napa County Airport."

The Napa County Airport. It's a private airport in the heart of wine country. It's a small airport, but an impressive one. Mostly smaller planes fly out of there, but a few larger jets. All privately owned and operated. I flew there with Belle once when we were working on her St. Helena home. I flew there with Belle. And Avett.

I feel a tightening in my chest even thinking of them. Of Owen's old boss, of his wife. Of the day (a lifetime ago) this all started.

"Can you be there by ten a.m.?" Patty asks.

"Yes."

"When you get there, head straight to the tarmac. No one should stop you if you look like you know where you're going."

"I do know, loosely, where I'm going. I've been there before."

"That's why we chose it."

We. I want to ask who she means by we. I want to ask at the same time that I know I can't. For all the reasons she can't answer.

"You'll be leaving from Runway 19R/1L. Tail number 82165. Are you writing this all down?"

"I'll remember."

"Fine. Be there at ten a.m. Don't be late, but don't come too early. You'll be met by the plane."

I don't ask the name of who is meeting me. I assume if she wanted to say the name, she would. I do ask her one thing though, so on that I can be clear. So I can be clear in terms of what I say to Bailey.

"Is it someone I know?" I ask. "Meeting us."

"Not who you hope," she says. "Not yet."

Not yet.

My heart pounds in my chest. Bailey watches me and I put the phone on speaker so she can hear too.

"If you run into any problems, go to the office and ask for Tami O'Sullivan. Tell her that you are with the Roberts party. Don't show anyone your ID. Tami will not ask for any form of ID, got it?"

"Okay."

"You really should be writing this down."

"Not necessary."

"Fine. I should go."

The First Time I Saw Him

I look at Bailey, who leans toward the phone, so Patty can hear what she needs to say.

"Patty," Bailey asks. "Have you seen him?"

Patty doesn't answer her, not at first. She clears her throat.

"We'll get into that later, okay? It's not the time, Bails . . ." she says, but she says it soft. Kind.

It's the voice Patty reserves for a person that she likes.

"I'm sorry about your grandfather, sweetheart," she says. "I know how close you guys were."

"Thank you," Bailey says. "Me too."

I take the phone off speaker, hold it to my ear.

"Anything else I need to know?" I ask.

"Nothing for now," she says. "I'll be at the gallery tomorrow until you're wheels up. Call if you need to. But only if you really need to."

"We can't thank you enough, Patty," I say.

"You shouldn't be thanking anyone yet," she says. "This is just getting started."

Alfred Hitchcock Lived in These Hills

The house in Santa Cruz isn't unfamiliar to me.

I visited Jules several times the year when she was teaching at the university there. And, each time, we drove out to this home in the heart of Scotts Valley—a gorgeous community in the upland slope of the Santa Cruz Mountains. All redwood trees and vineyards, hiking trails as far as the eye can see.

The owner hasn't only been Jules's close friend since graduate school, but he was also responsible for bringing her to teach at Santa Cruz in the first place. He is a tenured journalism professor here—not to mention the sole heir to a snack food empire, which explains how he's able to afford the stunning eighteen-acre estate up on one of Scotts Valley's most famed roads. It's a Tuscan-inspired estate complete with a gated courtyard, an infinity pool, and a working vineyard. Sweeping views in every direction.

The snack empire is how he's able to afford his beautiful house—and, more importantly, how he's able to afford the boat.

I tap in the code at the front gate and the steel doors swing open, revealing the large main house, lit up and glowing against the expanse.

It looks like he is home, many of the lights are on. It looks like he is inside with his partner and their kids. I can picture them sitting at the kitchen table, eating dinner, sharing a glance when they were notified that the gate was open. Then, before their kids noticed, they'd return their focus to their family.

I won't know for sure. I keep driving. I pull past the main house and continue down the driveway, which narrows, leading us past the vineyard and toward the back of the property and the pool house. The pool house, which is larger than any house I've ever lived in, waiting for us. Food in the refrigerator, fresh sheets on the bed. The keys to the slip and the boat and all its necessary documentation on the kitchen island.

I can see the awe on Bailey's face, despite the circumstances, at the scope of this estate, at its depth.

"It's only for the night," I remind her.

"Why's that?" Bailey says. "We could probably hide in different rooms here forever and no one would find us."

~

The refrigerator has been stocked for us with fruit, pasta, and roasted chicken from a local organic grocer.

We eat by the pool, Bailey dipping her legs in the water. We are exhausted from the day and ravenous for some nourishment, something warm and filling that doesn't come out of a shiny bag.

"It's so freaking pretty here," Bailey says. "You could almost forget it, you know? Why you're here."

I nod. "Not the worst thing."

"It has like a . . . historic vibe."

She isn't wrong. And it pulls me back to the first time I was here. So long ago—a weekend when I came to visit Jules and she was house-sitting. Before Owen. And long before I knew there was a time I'd be back here, like this.

I was walking the property with Jules, having an after-dinner glass of wine when she pointed out a gorgeous property perched on a hillside in the distance.

The First Time I Saw Him

Do you see that vineyard to the north over there? she asked. *That used to be Alfred Hitchcock's house.*

I debate sharing this with Bailey, who—if she was less on edge—would find it intriguing. Would hold it as further proof. *See? Told ya. Historic.*

Considering the mood she is in—a little frantic, her nails down to the stubs—I keep it to myself. I want to hold as much of this for her as I can, except what she absolutely must know for her safety.

It's the reason for all of this, after all, for everything I've fought so hard for: to let Bailey be twenty-two, as unburdened as possible, the way she deserves to be. The way Owen would want her to be.

So I tell her to go inside and take a long shower, wash the day off. That I'll clean up and meet her upstairs.

"You sure? I can help."

"I've got it," I say.

Bailey smiles, grateful. She heads inside, and I go back into the pool house kitchen and wash the silverware.

Then I take a seat at the island and pull out my laptop. There is a cordless phone on the island. There's a landline.

I power on my laptop in case I need to take notes.

At exactly 8:55, the landline rings. I pick it up quickly.

"You made it," Jules says.

It isn't exactly a question, but I answer anyway.

"We did," I say. "We're fine."

"Good, I'm relieved to hear it . . ." she says. "I'm at Frances."

Frances. Our favorite restaurant in the Castro. The restaurant where Owen and I had our wedding dinner. This is her way of letting me know that she is calling from their kitchen phone, as planned, that no one is going to be tracing this call. Her personal phone is off-limits, her work phone at the *San Francisco Chronicle* too. But no one will be thinking to trace a restaurant phone to find where Bailey and I are.

She is on a secure line for us to talk. And, still, we are both careful. We don't say anything specific about her friend's boat or Bailey's and my plan for tomorrow. I certainly don't say anything specific about Patty and Daniel and the flash drive. How the plan looks like it's shifting.

"I'm sorry, Hannah," Jules says. "I'm so sorry about Nicholas."

I feel that in my throat, like a weight, and it takes everything in me not to give in to it while Bailey is in the shower, while I can. Jules saying it out loud makes Nicholas's death feel more immediate—the way it feels more real when the person who knows you best acknowledges something you've lost.

Nicholas's face shifts forward in my mind, a spike of grief coming in fast and raw.

I clinch against it, bite it back—in part because I know what Nicholas would say, if he were here—the very thing I'm saying to myself. *Get Bailey to safety.*

So I push my pain down. I push it down and focus.

"What are you hearing at work?" I ask.

"That all signs point to a heart attack. Apparently, the coroner's initial conjecture is that he died in his sleep."

I nod as though she can see me, feeling a bit of relief to know he was sleeping. To hope that he didn't suffer.

"So . . . no sign of foul play?"

"Doesn't appear that way."

"Don't they have to wait for the autopsy?"

"Nicholas apparently, in his will, requested that there wouldn't be one." She pauses. "That's not uncommon. Certainly not at his age. And I have it from a reliable source that his bodyguard was the one that found him."

The First Time I Saw Him

"His regular bodyguard?" I say. And I think of Seth. Seth, who has always been the one Nicholas wanted with him. There would be comfort in knowing that he was there.

"I'll find out," she says. "It was confirmed that no one entered or exited the property at any point last night."

Last night. How was this all just twenty-four hours ago?

I look at my computer screen—click on the *Family* photo album. I flip through until I land on a photograph of Nicholas. It's an old photograph (at least two decades old), a far-younger Nicholas enjoying dinner with Kate and Charlie when they were still children at a beachfront restaurant in Hawaii. It's a beachfront restaurant that I recognize because Nicholas took us all there the year before last—Charlie and his boys; me and Bailey. It was the last trip we took with Nicholas before we all knew about his heart condition, before Bailey and I worried about him the way we have worried since.

It makes me smile, despite myself, remembering that vacation. And looking at a photograph of the much-younger version of Nicholas in the same place—his young children flanking either side of him: Charlie on one side, Kate on the other (Kate looking so much like Bailey), Nicholas looking so happy, his large arm draped over her shoulder.

The photograph captures a moment in which Nicholas feels so much like himself, a moment that encapsulates him—his arms around the people he loved most in this world, trying to hold them as tightly as he can.

It was almost as though I could feel Nicholas consider it just as the photograph was being taken. It was buried behind his smile: the knowledge that, one day, he wouldn't be able to hold them like this anymore.

"Word at the paper is that CNN is going to use Nicholas's death as a reason to do a special on the organization. A look back at their history and how they evolved into a where-they-are-today kind of thing. Focusing on Frank's legacy, the changing of the guard."

"The changing of the guard?" I ask.

"From what I'm hearing, Frank has taken a step back and is in the process of officially handing over the reins to his children," she says.

I think of what Nicholas has shared with me about Frank's children. There are six of them, in total. The youngest four, apparently, are spread out around the country—not particularly involved. But the oldest two are still in south Florida. A daughter named Quinn, and her younger brother Teddy.

"The daughter, especially, has apparently started playing a larger role."

That doesn't land correctly for me. If Frank had stepped back, and Quinn had stepped in, wouldn't Nicholas have known? Wouldn't he have shared that with me? Or had he known and chosen to keep it to himself? Maybe because he was worried too—that the man responsible for Bailey's and my safety was no longer the only boss?

Maybe because, like how I tried to do with Bailey, Nicholas was trying to shield me from some of that fear.

Grady's words pop to the forefront of my mind: *Everything has changed.*

And what he said next: *The organization isn't honoring the deal you two made . . . that you and Bailey would be safe. . . .*

"That must play into this," I say.

"Into what?" Jules asks.

"I had a visitor last night," I say. "An unexpected visitor. Which may be leading to my making a potential shift. To the plan."

She's quiet. Because she knows what I'm not saying. That the visitor was Owen. I don't have to explain beyond that. Jules understands, better than anyone, that there is only one reason I would shift

The First Time I Saw Him

everything I've been planning. There is only one reason that I would choose a different path in the eleventh hour. Because the eleventh hour could possibly take us back to Owen. Could possibly take my kid back to her father.

"What do you need me to do?" she asks.

"I may need to come back here," I say. "I need this window to stay open."

"Of course. I'll take care of that." She pauses. "When?"

"A day or two. I just don't know yet."

I don't answer her beyond that. I don't need to. She'll let her friend know I may be back. She'll let her friend know no details beyond that, until and unless it becomes absolutely necessary.

"Keep me close, okay?" Jules says.

"Always," I say.

Then we hang up.

~

I go upstairs to find Bailey in the primary bedroom.

The bed is enormous, and Bailey is already lying on a corner of it. Her sweats are on. Her hair is damp from the shower.

And her burner phone, the one I had waiting for her, is in her hands. I don't have to double-check that she isn't texting anyone. Not Shep or her friends or her boss. She doesn't need me to tell her that she can't do that. She knows what she can and can't do.

"You okay?" I ask instead.

"Yeah, I think so," she says. "The shower helped."

She pulls her legs up so I can scooch onto the base of the bed. I lie down, perpendicular to her, holding her ankle.

"Good," I say.

"Can we both sleep in here tonight?" she asks.

I offer her a smile, trying not to make a big deal about her asking me to stay close. But it still catches me, fills my chest up. Especially now that we live apart, these moments are fewer and further between—as they're supposed to be. But I treasure them when they come. I treasure the knowledge that, against the odds, it gets to be me. I get to be the one that makes Bailey feel safe.

"Please!" I say. "I almost got lost on my way up here to find you."

She gives me a laugh, it's a small laugh, but her first all day. I feel it move through me. A little found joy.

"How about you?" she asks.

"How about me?"

"You doing all right?"

She is worried. I can hear it. She is worried about me.

"No no no," I say. "No worrying about me. That's not allowed, kid."

She rolls her eyes, and I know she wants to point out that she's not a kid anymore. But she knows that would be useless. She knows that I'll push back. I'll remind her that I was my grandfather's kid until the day he died. That I will resist all of her instincts to take care of me, just like he resisted all of my instincts to take care of him. It's the great blessing of my life—that I get to be the one to take care of her.

"I keep looking at my phone, expecting a million texts from my boss," she says. "She must actually be losing her mind that she can't reach me."

"Sorry about that."

"Don't be," she says. "Her not being able to reach me is the only upside of this whole fucking mess . . ."

I give her a smile.

"But I can't stop thinking about how I had to work last Sunday

The First Time I Saw Him

until almost midnight, and so I missed Grandpa's weekly call. I missed our last call. That just seems . . . I don't know . . . so fucked-up."

"Bails, there was no way for you to know."

"No, I know." She pauses. "But I'm having trouble figuring out when we last spoke before that. I don't know for sure. I mean, without my phone, there's no way to really know. But, whenever it was, he was telling me about this cartoon he saw in the *New Yorker*," she says. "Only Grandpa would actually like . . . try to explain a cartoon as opposed to texting the photo of it . . ."

I nod, not saying what I know to be true. That the reason Nicholas didn't just send a screenshot, but walked Bailey through it, was that he knew that Bailey loved *New Yorker* cartoons. And talking about them was a way to keep Bailey on the phone—it was a way to get to hear her laugh. The way I knew he loved that laugh.

"It was a funny one. It's the one where the father takes his kid out fishing. Did you see it?"

"No, I don't think so," I say.

"Okay, well, the kid catches this tiny fish and the father tells his kid to smear any witnesses that said the fish wasn't big. I'm not explaining it great, but I'm telling you it was funny."

"You're taking on your grandfather's role."

"Exactly," she says. "Anyway, Grandpa was laughing so hard. Which made me laugh so hard. And I don't know, maybe it was the kid and dad fishing together, like Dad and I used to do, but . . . I just thought Dad would love that cartoon too. And so I told Grandpa that, you know? I said, *Dad would love this*. It just came out before I thought about it."

"About what?"

She shakes her head, struggling to bite back her tears. "That Grandpa was probably mad that I'd bring up Dad to him."

"He wasn't mad."

"Then why did he get off the phone so quickly?"

She looks away from me, the tears spilling out, no matter how she is trying to stop them.

All of it is catching up to her at once: her sadness that she is without Nicholas now, her incredible sadness that he isn't here to hold her close to him and tell her that it's okay between them. That, with their kind of love, it's forever okay.

"Bailey," I say. "Nicholas was never, not for a moment of his life, anything but totally in love with you. Don't spend a second worrying about that."

"I just don't know why I had to bring him up."

"Because your father is who you always want to bring up. Me too." I shrug. "That's love."

"But why aren't *you* mad?"

I look at her, confused. "At Nicholas?"

"At Dad," she says. "I mean, I know we've talked about all of this. But how does it not catch up to you? Like, here we are again, and you just don't seem mad that he . . ."

"Put us in this position?"

She nods.

I hold her eyes. Those beautiful eyes, bright with tears.

I want to tell her that getting mad isn't going to get me anywhere that I want to be, but that's not the whole truth. The whole truth is closer to this: Being mad at someone is almost a luxury. It means they are there to hear it. What I am, still, is figuring out if that's a luxury we're going to have. What we are both doing now is figuring out if that is something we get to hope for.

I reach over, wipe away her tears.

"The thing is . . ." I say. "I know your father. And I'm guessing that being hard on him is a waste of time, considering how hard he is probably still being on himself."

"So . . . you're not mad?"

I think of Owen, in front of me twenty-four hours before. What was living there underneath my happiness at seeing him last night? What was living beneath my confusion as to what he was doing there? Was it anger?

No. It was more like something else. Something like hope that there would be a time where he'd be safely in front of me—and that would get to be the work between us again. What it means to forgive.

"No," I said. "Not mad. Not just yet."

The Middle of the Night Tells a Different Story

After Bailey falls asleep, I crawl out of bed and walk out to the terrace off the bedroom. I close the glass door quietly, careful not to wake her.

Across the way, I see the main house. All the lights are now off. Everyone in there is asleep for the night. The landscape of this estate—this gorgeous, endless acreage—silent except for the trees and the soft nighttime breeze. The mountain air fresh and unburdened.

I lean against the railing, the chill rising on my arms. I push up against that air, let it steady me, trying to help it pull down the tired. I'm so very tired at the same time that I know sleep isn't in the cards for me, not tonight. Not with everything moving through my mind about what is coming next.

I brace myself as I pull out my phone, click on CNN's latest news. I scan their home page for more updates about Nicholas Bell's passing. I'm waiting for a journalist to make the connection to Owen: for the doorman at Nicholas's building to report that Owen was there last night, or for one of their crime experts to come forward and drudge up the history between Owen and Nicholas, the history that sent Nicholas to jail—when Owen turned state's evidence.

But there's nothing about Owen. I have to search to even find anything about Nicholas. Other events are taking over the headlines and breaking news chyrons, taking over the social media gawking.

There's a plane crash in Reno; a celebrity divorce; a beloved rock band announcing a new US tour schedule.

Nicholas, just like that, already (and quite literally) yesterday's news. The twenty-four-hour news cycle seemingly done with him entirely. The incendiary headlines are done with him before they even pulled Owen into it.

I feel a moment of relief, but before I can even breathe into it, I feel something else. I feel it in the quiet.

I go over what Jules told me: cable news is prepping a longer story on the organization. Owen will find his way there. Owen will find his way there, Nicholas, all of us. Nicholas was an integral part of the organization for decades. He was chief legal counsel, an unofficial consigliere to leadership—and, most critically, a trusted advisor to Frank himself. There is no way that Nicholas escapes having his story told in a larger way in conjunction with theirs.

So I can't deny that this is just a small respite from seeing Nicholas's name in the news again, from seeing Owen's name alongside it.

And that is the least of it. I know it in my gut.

Because the other thing Jules said keeps pushing its way to the forefront of my mind, more immediate and more terrifying: *There's been a changing of the guard.*

Mirroring what Grady said: *Everything has changed.*

Which leads to a question about the past that I need to figure out the answer to—a question that will influence how I go about keeping us safe in the present: What, exactly, did it change from?

And why, exactly, did any mercy—for me, for Bailey—need to go with it?

Forty-Three Years Ago

The best advice Nicholas's father ever gave him was this: *Never let fear make your decisions.*

Of course, his father offered this advice shortly before Nicholas's seventh birthday, as justification for his own decision to head off for a new life with a girlfriend out in California, while opting to leave Nicholas and his little brother and their mother behind in Texas. Despite that (and, also, because of it) the advice stuck. And it was the first thing Nicholas thought of when he agreed to meet Frank.

Because, if Nicholas was being honest, fear was *why* he said yes. He was thirty-one years old with a family to support and crushing law school and college debt. The kind of debt that didn't get paid off from a civil servant job. And he feared what would happen if he said no to a crime boss. Would he be killed for that? Did these kinds of people kill for things like that? Would it all lead to Nicholas inadvertently abandoning his family, just like his father had? Nicholas had organized his life to do the opposite of his father.

And still we can do tricks in our minds, can't we? Especially when the impossible seeps in. Which is exactly what Nicholas did. He convinced himself that it wasn't fear guiding him. In fact, he convinced himself it was closer to the opposite.

It was the promise of freedom.

Meredith was working full-time as a guidance counselor and leaving the kids with her mother, which she hated. But they needed

Meredith's salary unless Nicholas left the Austin public defender's office.

He was making a difference there, wasn't that the point? But now there were other points. Meredith and their children. The main points. Nicholas would do whatever was needed for them. He interviewed for a partner track position at a tony criminal law firm. It would mean a move to Houston, where the criminal law firm had their headquarters. Meredith would be able to stay home with the kids, but she would be far from Austin and her parents. It was a trade they were gearing up to make, if Meredith decided she wanted it. She couldn't seem to decide. She was trading the guilt of not taking care of her young kids with abandoning her unwell father.

This was where they were, perched at that inflection point, with two realities that weren't quite working for them. Being presented with a third reality. Because of Harris Gray.

Harris Gray was a young man who had been caught selling prescription pills at a fraternity party on UT-Austin's campus, and whose case had been assigned to Nicholas. It was an open-and-shut case for the state. Harris was caught with the drugs in hand.

But Nicholas had managed to get it dismissed.

This was why he loved his job. He loved helping people who needed it. Who needed it more than a young kid like Harris, who grew up with nothing and got out over his skis to correct that? Nicholas thought that Harris would take his second chance and do things differently. That was until Nicholas learned that Harris worked for the organization.

Every criminal lawyer in the United States was familiar with the organization and the family at its helm. It wasn't a crime syndicate the way folks traditionally thought of crime syndicates: narcotics and prostitution, loan sharking. Extortion. Murder.

The First Time I Saw Him

Frank Campano Pointe II did things differently from the generations before him. He and his leadership team operated the organization out of South Florida, focused on more sophisticated revenue streams like international online gaming and brokerage fraud. Most notably, they bulked up their OxyContin business long before their competitors saw the opening there.

That was where Harris Gray came in. Harris Gray—whose open-and-shut case Nicholas had managed to make less open-and-shut.

This is what led to a phone call from Frank himself. And a job offer from Frank. A job offer that would allow Nicholas to spend most of his time still taking on pro bono cases and helping out at the public defenders and staying in Austin. A job offer that would have Nicholas consulting on a high level with Frank's legal team when future criminal matters arose. A job offer that he wanted to discuss more in person. *No strings*, Frank had said.

Did Nicholas believe there were no strings? Not exactly, no. The very nature of agreeing to the meeting already involved strings. But if Nicholas had declined the invitation, that would be a different kind of string. The string connecting Nicholas to the organization was already in place as soon as Frank saw how good Nicholas was at his job—and as soon as Frank decided he wanted more of him. Because Frank was used to getting exactly what Frank wanted.

Never let fear make your decisions.

What about when fear and freedom started to feel like the same thing?

Frank flew Nicholas and Meredith to Miami on a private plane. It was going to be a three-day vacation, care of Frank, the only obligation was one face-to-face meeting.

It was the only time that Meredith had ever left her kids, except when her grandmother died. Meredith had flown to Italy, to her grandparents' small farm in Tuscany to bury her. Then she flew straight home. Less than three days.

Nicholas expected Meredith to pull out of the trip at the last moment. All the way to the airport it felt like it could go either way. She kept biting on her thumbnails, the way she did when she was thinking or nervous or both.

But something shifted in his wife when they drove through the airport gates, straight up to the tarmac, the private plane waiting for them. Even Nicholas was a little wooed. He had been on planes before but never on a private plane. Never on a plane just for him.

"Is this safe?" Meredith asked.

But she was already getting out of the car. She was already heading for the stairs and up to the private cabin and the glass of champagne waiting for her.

It was like watching a switch go on: She was enjoying herself, for the first time in a long time. And Nicholas loved seeing it.

At the airport in Miami, a black car was waiting. It drove Nicholas and Meredith to their oceanfront hotel to freshen up and then to the exit for Frank's compound on Fisher Island.

Fisher Island was a gated community that put most gated communities to shame. You needed to board a security-guarded ferry to even get to it. And you needed an invitation to even get on that ferry.

When the ferry arrived on the island, they were greeted by additional security who took them by golf cart down the palm tree–landscaped roads (lush residences, tropical plants, and windblown foliage) until they got to the far end of the island—where Frank's stunning house sat perched overlooking the Atlantic Ocean and Biscayne Bay.

It was the largest house on the island, but somehow the most welcoming with its blue shutters and flowers on the windowsills, a large oak door.

The First Time I Saw Him

Frank and his wife, Jenny, and their children were waiting for them in the sunroom with cocktails being stirred and bowls of olives and oven-warm rosemary nuts. And, of course, those ocean views.

Frank was only a few years older than Nicholas, but he could have been a decade older. He was dressed in a pressed button-down shirt and khakis, relaxed loafers.

Jenny was in a white sundress, no shoes. And very pregnant. Pregnant for the fourth time. *Twins this go-round*, she said.

Their kids were bouncing around the sunroom and the backyard just beyond it, like a photograph of a happy family. There was an adorable blond and curly-haired daughter named Quinn, and her two younger brothers, Teddy and Dominic.

Jenny reached for Meredith, took her by the shoulders. "You're not going to believe this, but I grew up not too far from you and your husband here," she said.

"Really?" Meredith said, unable to hide her surprise.

"Your maiden name is Smith, yes?"

"Yes."

"My maiden name is Delaney," she said. Then she turned to Nicholas. "Your brother Sam was a grade behind me, I think. Or two grades maybe? I can't remember . . . but I recognized your name straightaway. And I knew you from the football team. Everyone knew you from the football team. What are the odds, right?"

A Texas city of eighty thousand people, a high school of fewer than five hundred. Nicholas and Meredith and Jenny among the few who managed to find their way out. To find their way to somewhere better. To, somehow, find their way to each other.

What were the odds? Not high, Nicholas knew. And yet, the older he was getting, the more it felt to him like further proof. We end up where we start.

So even if it didn't all feel destined, it certainly did make Jenny seem knowable, familiar. It made Frank seem that way by association. Frank who was on the ground with his kids, tending to them in a way that was disarming to Nicholas—breaking apart LEGOs and zipping up a doll's dress.

This was the head of a crime empire? He seemed like a smitten family man.

Of course, though, you could be both.

The kids ran into the family room to watch *Superman II* on the VHS. And Jenny took Meredith's arm, locked it in her own, steering her out toward two Adirondack chairs on the far end of the backyard, to sip on white wine, to talk about friends they used to have in common. To start down the road they naturally seemed like they both wanted to be walking down.

And Nicholas was alone with Frank. Frank who'd been down on the floor playing with his kids.

In a moment, Frank would tell Nicholas to have a seat on one side of the sunroom table, Frank handing him a cocktail and sitting down across from him. In a moment, Frank would lean back in that chair and start the conversation he'd asked Nicholas to fly fifteen hundred miles to have in person.

Nicholas was ready for this. He expected Frank to lay out the case for why he should do this: Everyone deserved a fair defense; criminal defense lawyers represented criminals; Nicholas taking a few cases a year for the organization would mean he could keep doing the meaningful work he loved, for people who needed someone like him to care; the organization had in-house counsel, so this was more of a consulting role, which would allow Nicholas to stay near his home and take care of his family, and family (they could both agree, couldn't they?) was everything to them.

The First Time I Saw Him

But Frank didn't do any of that. He merely slid a folder across the table and waited for Nicholas to open it. Inside the folder was a list of every client the tony firm in Houston represented—the firm that had offered Nicholas a job.

Nicholas scanned the client list, the cases: corporations destroying the environment, hedge funders stealing retirement funds, sociopathic sons of billionaires. Rapists and murderers and extortionists. All the awful people that Nicholas would be expected to save, simply because they had the money to be saved. The people he'd have to fight for 120 hours a week. Until it killed him.

Nicholas looked up from the folder. It took a lot to surprise him and he was focused on not showing it, on not giving that away. Which might be why it didn't occur to Nicholas, until later that night, in his oceanfront hotel room, that he had no idea how Frank knew about the job offer in the first place.

But they were a step before all of that anyway. They were at the step where everything changed.

Frank stood up. And he put out his hand.

And Nicholas—he took it.

There's Always Time to Turn Back, But Which Way Is Back?

We are on the road by 6 a.m.

If we drive the most direct way, it would take us just over two hours—but that means tollbooths and cameras that I want to avoid.

So I take the longer way, continuing to hug the coast for as long as possible. Bailey is quiet in the car, but I can feel the intake of breath as we wind our way onto I-280—which takes us close to our familiar stomping grounds—a little too close to Sausalito. A little too close to her time with her father. To the last time she had her father.

I feel it catch in my own throat as we hit the Golden Gate Bridge, a bridge to a world I try not to let myself think about. But it comes crashing in, and I consider turning the car around. I consider telling Bailey this is a mistake—that we need to stick to going back to Santa Cruz. That we need to stick with my plan. Isn't this crazy, to switch now?

Except that it's also not crazy.

I turn to Bailey and I meet her eyes and I have faith it's not crazy. Owen would never lead Bailey into crazy. After all this time, he would only be coming back if we needed him to help ensure the opposite.

Maybe believing that makes me sounds delusional. But it doesn't matter how it sounds. It doesn't matter how it sounds or how it looks or what it seems like.

Because that's the thing about faith. Even if the world decides it looks crazy, it shows up for you in the moment that you need it most. The moment that you need faith to remind you that you know better.

That I know better.

This is when I keep going.

∼

At 8:55 a.m., we pull into the parking lot at a restaurant in a small office park, half a mile from the Napa County Airport.

We get two large coffees and split a breakfast burrito. We park at the far end of the lot and eat on a bench, facing the morning sun.

At 9:30, we take everything out of the trunk, the duffels and backpacks, and lock the car. For the last time.

Then we start the walk to Napa County Airport.

The road is windy, mostly quiet and flat, and thankfully not very busy. A truck passes by us, a couple of cars. I'm glad that there isn't much traffic to take notice of us—these two women walking with their bags on their backs, walking over train tracks, hugging the side of the dusty road.

But, even if they do notice us, it's still the best option. Even if our car isn't directly traceable to us, we can't leave it someplace where they might be looking for it. And I can't risk a taxi driver remembering the two women he dropped off at the small private airport. The two women who fit our description.

We round a corner, and suddenly the airport is visible, fifty feet ahead of us. You could almost miss it. You could almost miss the whole airport if you didn't know what you were looking for: a small building, a few makeshift bungalows. And, in the distance, a construction site—where they are building out a new airport hub.

"This is it?" Bailey says.

"This is it."

The First Time I Saw Him

We walk up to the sky service bungalow, a black gate beside it, leading to the tarmac. But instead of walking into that bungalow, and the small reception area inside, I lead Bailey straight through the open black gate, straight out to the tarmac.

We pass several of the smaller planes, moving wordlessly in the direction of the farthest runway. On the edge of which is the largest plane.

A long-range jet. It's big enough for twenty people, maybe more. But, apparently, it's there for just us.

The boarding stairs are down. There are three people standing beneath them. Three people in uniform who I can't make out just yet.

"Just follow my lead, okay?" I say.

Bailey nods. I can feel that she is nervous, so I take her hand and she lets me.

Then I keep walking us toward that large plane, with purpose, like this is something I'm used to doing. Like I'm familiar with this tarmac, with its rules, with planes waiting just for me.

"Can I help you?"

I hear a voice behind me, stopping me cold. We are a good fifty feet from the plane. I turn around to find a security guard in a golf cart. He is in his sixties in an orange vest with reflective stripes, a gun on his waistband.

I force my nicest smile—force myself to meet his eyes—to combat whatever suspicions he may be feeling.

"We're just heading to nineteen R," I say.

"Hop on. I'll drop you."

Bailey jumps in, a little too fast. "We're all set. Thanks."

His tilts his head, takes us in, suddenly suspicious. I look over at her and see her as he must—her skinny arms, balancing those heavy bags. Why on earth wouldn't she want the help? Most people coming through here expected it.

"You seem a bit weighed down with those bags," he says. "Let me drop you."

"No," she says. "All good."

He nods, but he reaches for his radio, probably ready to call someone to check our IDs, to look further into what we're doing here. He reaches for that radio on his holster. By his gun.

I move toward him.

"You know what?" I say. "My daughter here can speak for herself. I learned as soon as I turned forty, you don't turn down a lift . . ."

The security guard gives me a small laugh, liking this joke. Liking the chance to be helpful. His hand leaves the remote and he reaches out to make room for my bags on the back seat of the golf cart.

I hop onto the golf cart, sit down next to him.

Bailey gives me a look and I meet her eyes, trying to convey to her that this is the best choice. The only choice. She reluctantly gets into the golf cart's rear-facing row, holding her bag tightly on her lap.

The guard swings the golf cart back into drive, moving us in the direction of the apron, the large plane, takeoff.

"Where is today's destination?" he asks.

"That's a birthday surprise for the young lady behind you," I say.

"Ah," he says. "Lucky kid."

"Not so much a kid anymore as she is quick to remind me . . ."

"Can you not talk about me like I can't hear you?" Bailey says. She sounds surly, but I know she is leaning into what I'm doing here—adding this security guard to it. To our side.

"She sounds just like my two," he says. "Just celebrated my youngest's thirty-fifth. And let me tell you, I still see him as three years old."

"I hear grandkids help?" I ask.

"More than anything."

The First Time I Saw Him

He offers me a smile and drives us the rest of the way to the plane in silence. I keep the smile plastered to my face, watching him. I don't breathe though. I don't breathe until we are off the golf cart again and standing by the plane's boarding stairs.

The three people I saw from a distance are now a few feet from us, and visible to me: a flight attendant; a young pilot who I don't recognize in his uniform; and the other pilot—slightly older—also in his uniform. This other pilot, who I do recognize.

Daniel.

Daniel, who moves toward me. "Ms. Roberts," he says. "Always nice to see you."

He reaches out his hand to shake mine—somewhere between formal and cordial. Somewhere between knowing me and working for me. And it occurs to me that he is trying to strike a balance—to convey that we've been here several times before, boarding a private plane, on a chartered flight I have hired him to pilot for me.

Daniel motions toward the flight attendant. "Sally will be taking care of you today," he says. "And this is my copilot, Ryan."

The younger pilot, Ryan, gives us a nod and walks on board. Sally stays by Daniel's side.

"Thank you for having your assistant send over the passports," Daniel says. "That expedited everything, and we should be ready to get going shortly."

Sally hands me the passports, and I force a smile. I don't dare look at Bailey, who is keeping her eyes down. Bailey who knows it wasn't us who sent passports anywhere. Bailey who, like me, is wondering not only where these passports were sent over from, but also what the passports even say.

Last name Roberts, apparently.

"After you," Daniel says.

He smiles and turns toward the stairs. He motions for Bailey and me to follow Sally onto the plane.

I let Bailey take the lead. I follow her up the stairs and into the main cabin. A gorgeous main cabin: a couch to our right, four plush chairs around a dining table on the left side, a bar area behind that.

Bailey turns back toward me, and I can see it in her eyes. Despite the strangeness of all of this, she is still wooed by it. She has never been on a private plane before. I have been on a few with clients, but nothing like this—not a full-size jet of this magnitude.

"*Bananas*," Bailey mouths.

I nod back. *I know.*

Then I turn toward Daniel. He stands at the front of the cabin, Sally preparing a tray of drinks behind him in the galley.

"As I'm guessing you might remember, Ms. Roberts, flying regulation calls for two pilots on board if you are entering international airspace, so Ryan will be joining us for the duration."

International air space. A knot constricts in my chest. *Where* in international airspace?

But Daniel shakes his head—quickly, almost imperceptibly. It's as if he is warning me not to ask any questions. Questions he can't answer because Ryan may hear. Or Sally. Or someone else entirely.

"We'll be stopping for fuel at Teterboro, but I don't anticipate we'll need to deboard during that process. I'll certainly let you know if that changes . . ."

Daniel stops himself there, not saying the rest. He doesn't say out loud what I hear in his pause: If we do have to deboard, this could get more complicated. This international destination we are supposed to be heading toward potentially derailed.

"Any questions for me, just let Sally know."

A million, I want to say. A million questions.

The First Time I Saw Him

"None I can think of," I say.

"Very good. Wheels up in ten."

Then Daniel heads into the cockpit, closing the door behind him. Bailey and I stare at each other silently.

But I feel Sally's eyes on me, watching me. So I start to move—the way I would move if any of this were normal, if settling in were actually an option.

I drop our bags on the couch and then take a seat at the table, Bailey sitting down across from me. I click on my seat belt, motion for Bailey to do the same. I reach across the table to squeeze her hand, to try and help her relax, just as Sally places a large cheese board in front of us.

"I've got a few pre-takeoff bites here for you to enjoy," she says. "Can I get y'all something to drink?"

I shake my head. "We're fine. Thank you."

"Great, then just settle in."

This is when I look up. I look up and notice it on the front wall. There is a map with the flight plan on it. A little plane icon, our little plane apparently.

There's a map of America. The Atlantic Ocean. Europe. And the twelve hours and fifteen minutes we are about to embark on, airborne. Flying from APC to LBG.

LBG. It takes me just a second to process it.

LBG is the airport code for Le Bourget.

A small, private airport that I'm not unfamiliar with.

In Paris.

You Can't Plan for What You Can't Plan For

The last time I was in Paris, I was with Owen.

We were there for a belated honeymoon, almost a year after we got married. We spent six nights there, just the two of us. Bailey was spending a week at Interlochen, a performing arts camp in Michigan. A camp for which she had to audition—a camp she would have moved into if Owen had let her.

We dropped her at camp and then went straight back to the airport. Straight to France from there.

It was the longest Owen had ever been away from Bailey.

The longest the two of us had been away together alone. It was much-needed time alone together, especially when those were the days Bailey could barely stand to look at me. I remember our last exchange when I left her at Interlochen was me telling her that I couldn't wait to hear all about her experience there, and Bailey just staring at me blankly. *Sure*, she'd said.

Now, Bailey eyes me, and I know she is making the same calculation. Especially because she saw it too. Just yesterday. She saw the folder on the flash drive, marked *O&H Honeymoon*. She knows we spent it in Paris.

I motion for her to come sit beside me, on the same side of the small table, as I power on the laptop, inserting the flash drive.

And I go immediately to that photo album.

I don't need the photo album to remind me, but the photographs hit me just the same: that first day, walking through Luxembourg Gardens, letting the fresh air and rich coffee fight off the jet lag. The next day at the Musée d'Orsay. There's a photograph of one of Picasso's paintings, *Ulysses and sirens*. Did we see that in Paris? I don't remember seeing it in Paris . . .

But I do remember that night, and the perfect dinner at Le Voltaire on the Left Bank: omelets and french fries and ice-cold martinis, the moon showing off over the Seine. Owen included a photograph of me holding that martini, smiling at him in the way that only Owen made me smile.

I pull up the last photograph, a knot rising in my throat as Bailey zooms in, Owen and I coming into sharp focus. We were taking in the sunset on our hotel balcony—the Eiffel Tower in the distance. Owen kissing my neck, while he held the camera out, capturing both of us. When it was both of us.

And I remember the conversation we had later that night. It was that night, I'm fairly certain. He asked me if I could imagine living there. He confessed that he'd had a secret fantasy to move to Paris when he was in college. He imagined spending his days on the Left Bank, teaching at the Sorbonne. He'd even studied French, had become proficient, just in case it turned into more than a dream.

I look up and meet Bailey's eyes. But I won't let myself say it out loud—not to Bailey. I won't let myself think it. Not until he is actually in front of us again. Not until I know whether it's real.

This could be the place where he's figured it out.

How we get to be safe.

~

I must have fallen asleep.

I'm not entirely surprised I did. I didn't sleep at all last night.

The First Time I Saw Him

What is surprising is that it's the shaking of the plane that wakes me. The shaking of the plane as we are descending—almost, in fact, on the ground.

Bailey is asleep next to me, her head on my shoulder. I rub my eyes, still groggy, and look out the window as the wheels touch down.

I feel a drumbeat starting in my head, loud. It makes me uneasy.

Because I should have been ready for it. I should have been waiting for it. I look over at the flight plan. According to the map, it's not New Jersey that we've landed in. Not Teterboro as planned.

It's Miami.

I feel that in my chest, the drumbeat getting louder. Miami is the home of Fisher Island. Home base of the organization.

The last place—the very last place—I want to be. The last place I want Bailey to be.

"What's going on?" I say.

I say it a little too loudly, Sally looking up from where she is sitting in a jump seat in the galley—Bailey stirring awake.

I'm up, out of my seat, Bailey staring up at me.

"What's happening?" she asks.

I don't answer her. I look out the window, trying to scan who is heading toward the plane. There's a fuel truck (is it really a fuel truck?), several airport personal trailing behind it. They are all coming our way. The boarding stairs to the plane are not yet down, but they will be down any moment.

They will be down any moment unless I do something.

"I need to talk to the pilot," I call out to Sally. "Now."

Then I'm reaching for my burner phone, before they reach the plane, tapping out Grady's number.

I'm on the last digit—the very last digit—when Daniel walks out of the cockpit. He is walking toward me.

"Ms. Roberts? Is everything okay?"

"What are we doing in Miami?"

My tone is sharp, almost hostile. And I can see Daniel react to it, his brow tightening.

"We ran into a bit of weather," he says.

A bit of weather? Wouldn't a bit of weather have taken us somewhere closer to New York than Miami? Shouldn't we be stopping somewhere like Pennsylvania? Delaware at the farthest?

"All the way along the Eastern Seaboard?"

"Unfortunately, yes."

My heart starts racing faster. Who knows exactly what Daniel has been told: Daniel, who might not even understand that the plane being diverted here could be a setup. Or worse (unlikely, but worse), Daniel, who could have made a deal with the organization, selling out Owen. Selling Bailey and me out along with him.

"OPF can attend to us immediately," Daniel says. "They were the only airport who could. This will ensure we stay on time for your arrival to Paris, which I'm sure is your primary concern here . . ."

He says this last part loudly, as if saying it for Sally. Sally, who is now standing in the galley, pretending not to listen, but moving closer to us. Moving closer and clearly listening. He says this part *for* Sally, so she thinks I'm just another entitled passenger—not someone suspicious.

I look back out the window. The fuel truck is nearly beside the plane now. I'm running out of time. This is the moment to decide. If I call Grady now—if I tap the call button—then someone will come and help. I can keep the plane doors locked until they get here. I can hold my ground until they send us someone safe.

Someone safe to get us out of here. But someone who probably won't be taking us any closer to Owen.

The First Time I Saw Him

I turn back to Daniel, his hands folded in front of him, but one hand is shaking. I can see it shaking. And I see it in his eyes—what he wants me to understand. This wasn't the plan. This wasn't his plan, at least. That he, like me, is nervous about what it means that we've been diverted here.

Daniel is flying us to Paris because he can. Because he wants to help us, to help Owen. Because his brother is Owen's best friend. But beyond that, Daniel is out of his depth.

It nearly undoes me. I look down at my phone, zero in on the call button. Then I look over at Bailey. Bailey, who is staring back at me.

I've shielded her the best I can, but she knows enough to know that Miami is not good. She knows that the organization's upper management is based out of here. She knows enough to know this is the last place we want to be.

This is the thing about organizing your life the way I do—about knowing that you are only safe when you are completely prepared. When you are the one who takes control. In the rare moment where you aren't in control, you feel like you are giving someone else the chance to undo it: all the ways you work to protect her.

"*What the fuck?*" Bailey says.

I put my hand on her shoulder. I put my hand on her shoulder and I try to calm her—to let her know I've got this.

I try to believe that myself.

"No one deplanes," I say. "And the plane door stays closed, understood? So that we can take off as quickly as possible."

Daniel offers a small nod. "Understood."

Then, he heads back to the cockpit—past Sally, who will certainly be telling her new boyfriend later about the entitled woman she had on board today. Sally, who I pray will have the opportunity to say this.

You make a million decisions. You make a million decisions and one of them can undo you. One of them can save you, but any one of them can undo you. Which decision will this be?

"Grandpa said we should never come to Miami," Bailey whispers. "Isn't that the one thing he said?"

I nod. "I know."

My heart cracks in my chest, thinking of Nicholas. Nicholas, who I still can't believe is gone. Nicholas, who would be so upset that I've allowed his granddaughter to end up here, even for a moment. I can feel his arm on my shoulder, I can hear what he'd say if he were here: *We need to get her out of this.*

I sit back down next to her. And I put my arm around her, looking out the small airplane window at the fuel trucks and all the ground workers—at everyone starting to come closer to us.

"Mom," she says. "What do we do?"

"At the moment?" I say. "I think we pray."

Thirty-Eight Years Ago

"I pray that I'm wrong," Frank said. "But I don't think I am."

"No," Nicholas said. "I don't think so."

They were on a trip in Europe, in a small town in the South of France that Nicholas hadn't even known existed. It was a town called Cap Ferrat. The two families were vacationing together, staying in the most beautiful home that Nicholas had ever been in. It was an eighteenth-century Mediterranean villa with a clay tile roof and sunlit balconies and a pool hugging the edge of the coast. Frank's treat, of course.

Even with what Frank paid Nicholas, he couldn't afford a night in this villa, let alone eight. But Frank loved sharing this with Nicholas's kids, who he viewed as family, the closer they were all getting. Charlie and Katie were playing in the pool with the other kids. Jenny and Meredith dipping their feet in the water, talking about how they should make this a yearly tradition. What a way to ring in a New Year. Champagne and a rocky beach, the Mediterranean stretched out before them. Even more than the beauty of their surroundings there was this: everyone happy. Together, all of them. And happy.

Except for Frank.

The organization was back in the news, which Frank hated. He organized his business differently from his father—and from his father-in-law before that. He organized it to stay out of the news as much as possible.

And yet . . . here they were.

Six of the organization's associates had been arrested in a sting operation in New York. Charges included racketeering, conspiracy, violent extortion, assault. Arson.

It was all connected to the demolition industry—an old stronghold in the organization's business, a holdout from when Frank's father was still running things. These associates, all six of them, had thirty-year tenures in the organization—and were really his father's men. They were playing by the old rules of engagement.

"So we agree," Frank said.

"On what exactly?"

Even though Nicholas knew. He knew what was coming before Frank said it. He'd felt it coming for a long time.

"You know I hate to ask you to take lead on this, Nick . . ." Frank said. "You know I hate it."

"But you're asking me to take lead on this?"

Frank didn't answer at first. If Nicholas didn't step in, it would be Bobby and his team running point. Bobby had been with the organization for nearly as long as the associates that were causing this latest round of trouble. Bobby was a good lawyer. He wasn't as good as Nicholas though.

At the same time, Bobby was willing to do things that Nicholas wouldn't. He was willing to cross lines that Nicholas wouldn't.

Still, Nicholas was moving closer to the most important line, wasn't he? The line he swore he wouldn't cross. Frank and his children were splashing in the pool together, their wives sipping their sparkling pink wine. Their fates were intertwined.

Nicholas had a thought, in that moment—as clear as anything he'd ever known in his life. If he agreed to this—this could be it. The last time he could even see the line.

The First Time I Saw Him

"They're coming for me, Nicky, you know that," Frank said. "That's their strategy here . . ."

Nicholas couldn't disagree with Frank on that. If this case didn't get shut down (if Nicholas wasn't able to shut it down), it would give the FBI ammunition to get closer to the leadership. To get closer to Frank himself. Sometimes that boost was enough. You think you're making progress and that is just enough to propel things forward—to help you find the threads to get the rest of the way there.

"I can't move to Miami, Frank."

"No one is asking that. I would never ask you that."

That was cold comfort, Nicholas almost said out loud. Because, really, Frank wasn't asking him this either. He was just waiting for Nicholas to catch up.

Their kids were in the pool. Their wives were side by side.

How many ways, after all, were there not to say no?

Less Than Friendly Skies

We are on the ground for forty-two minutes.

Forty-two minutes, exactly. I hold the phone the entire time. I keep my eyes glued to the window. I watch the fuel truck. The men on the ground. I watch anyone getting too near to the airplane door.

I have mapped out a plan just in case they do. I have a plan to distract whoever comes in the front door while I get Bailey to safety. If they come up the stairs, I'll move Bailey to the cockpit. I'll lock her in there. I'll lock myself out.

I'll convince them to do it. I'll convince them to take me. I'll hand over the flash drive. I'll hand them anything and everything for them to leave her alone. I'll do what it takes to keep her free.

"They're just about finished," Daniel says.

I look up to see that he has come out of the cockpit. I give him a nod and turn back out to the fuel truck. The fuel truck that is getting ready to pull away. No one jumping off. No one, at all, making a move toward the plane door.

I turn back to Bailey, it starting to creep in, something like relief. But the only kind of relief I know now—the only kind I've known since Owen first disappeared. Temporary relief. Tightrope relief: the kind that must be navigated carefully until the next thing threatens to derail you. Threatens to cost you your balance.

"We're safe," she says.

It's a question as much as she wants it to be a statement.

But I nod, wanting her to believe that's true. And I don't volunteer the rest of it—the part that she doesn't need to hear. That, at the moment, I'm more certain than before that we are not safe.

Even if we're going to get out of Miami in one piece, it's still coming for us.

I know that it's coming for us.

Something that I won't be able to stop.

~

I don't sleep the rest of the way to Paris.

I open my laptop again and study the news. A few smaller outlets are still focusing on Nicholas, but there is nothing on Owen.

I flip over to the flash drive, culling through the photographs in each album, going back to *Hannah's Work*.

There are several photos of my larger pieces, but the only photograph with any people in it is the selfie of the two of us at that early exhibition.

It took place at a gallery in Los Alamos—a small town not too far from Santa Barbara. I loved Los Alamos, in part because it had reminded me of where I grew up in Tennessee—rustic and serene, farmland as far as the eye could see.

After the exhibition that night, Owen joked that we could move there after Bailey graduated. *If that's what you want, I'll follow you there*, he'd said. *Really, I'll follow you anywhere.*

I zoom back out, the memory cutting too hard.

But it sparks something in me, and I shift over to the album of France again, culling the entire *O & H Honeymoon* album. I'm not only looking for clues, but I'm also looking for the opposite.

What isn't adding up in what Owen sent me? What doesn't belong in this album, the way that the photograph of Daniel didn't add up in the Sausalito folder? The way that including that exhibition in Los Alamos sticks out in the work folder?

Because maybe that's what I should be following. What does Owen need me to know about what sticks out?

The *Ulysses and sirens* painting.

Picasso's famous painting of the *Odyssey*. I come back to that. Because I'm more and more certain that we didn't see that in person—not together. Not on that trip.

I do a quick search for the painting, and sure enough we wouldn't have seen it, not in Paris. The painting's not in Paris.

It's located at Musée Picasso Antibes—in the South of France. Why would Owen include a photograph of that, for me to find here?

"Did you get some rest?"

I look up, startled, to find Daniel standing over me. I flip my laptop closed and take a breath, doing a quick scan of the cabin. Sally is nowhere to be seen—not in the cabin or the galley. Sally is apparently in the restroom, Daniel taking the opportunity to come out of the cockpit to talk to me.

"A little."

"Good. You'll need it. We're about to start our descent."

He offers a smile, but it's forced, uncomfortable. I realize he feels like we can't discuss any of this. Even with Sally in the restroom. Even with Ryan in the cockpit. He wants to deliver us to Paris in one piece, and he wants to be done with his part of this.

Except for this. The one thing that he has to convey to me. The message he was instructed to deliver.

"So . . . will this be your first time at La Réserve?"

I look up at him. That's where we stayed during our honeymoon—Owen and I. That's where we stayed during those magical six nights.

It's a hotel in the 8th arrondissement. Small and intimate. So small that you could miss the hotel entirely, if you didn't know where you were going to look for it. Our last night in Paris, Owen said that we should make it a tradition—our tradition—to spend our anniversaries there. *We'll come back*, he said. *I promise you.*

Then again, he promised me a lot of things.

"No," I tell Daniel. "Not the first."

Before I can ask for any other details, Sally steps out of the bathroom and Daniel nods in her direction.

"You may want to wake your daughter," he says to me. He holds his gaze on Sally. "We'll be on the ground soon enough."

"Thank you," I say. "For everything."

"Pleasure," he says.

Then, as though we are strangers—which, in a way, we are—he walks away.

Forty Keys

"Not the way I thought I'd see the Eiffel Tower for the first time," Bailey says. "But okay . . ."

"Pretty spectacular, no?"

She nods. "Not bad."

We are in the back of a taxi, on the way to the hotel, Paris laid out before us, its beauty like a magic trick: the Eiffel Tower, and the bridges glistening in the midday sun, the museums along the river.

The taxi turns down Avenue Matignon and drops us in front of Hôtel Le Bristol—a historic hotel not far from the Champs-Élysées. From the Arc de Triomphe. It's a larger hotel than La Réserve—more well known—and feels like a safe place to be dropped. If someone is monitoring where we went from the airport—if someone manages to figure out we are people that should be monitored.

I pay the driver and we walk through Le Bristol's revolving doors, past the six doormen and into the magnificent lobby. Antique chandeliers and lavish white tile floors—classically French architecture in every direction.

We head through the lobby, and past the parlor for breakfast and high tea—before circling back around, slipping out one of the lobby's side doors.

I start walking quicker, weaving us through the crowds, in and out of traffic, toward where we are going—a half a mile down the street to Avenue Gabriel, and the small entrance that will lead us into La Réserve.

"Hey, don't turn around now, but . . ." Bailey says as we move at a brisk clip down the street. "There's a guy behind us, with a beard . . . black hat, green army jacket . . . I think he is following us."

I feel my heart pick up a beat, turn back to take a peek in his direction. I pretend like I'm looking at a store across the street, but watch him out of my peripheral view.

He is too far behind us for me to make out his face, but I see his thick beard. I see his jacket. He does seem to be moving at a steady clip, weaving in and out of people as quickly as we are.

"When did you first see him?"

"He walked out of the hotel the same time we did," she says. "Or . . . right after we did. I'm sure."

I nod, not doubting Bailey on that. She has become schooled in sensing when something feels off—when someone does. I have done my best to help school her. But, even if she is correct, there could still be a million reasons why this man is rushing down the Paris streets in the same direction we are. A million reasons that have nothing to do with us.

Still, when a door to a boutique opens, I push past the woman walking out—Bailey and I moving inside quickly, ducking behind a clothes rack. It's a children's boutique—pink and yellow tutus standing between us and the street.

We stay out of sight. And wait for him to pass. I want to see what he does, while we are no longer in view. Is he trying to find us? Or is he moving as quickly as he can in whatever direction he is going?

When he does pass, he isn't looking any which way. He is only looking straight ahead, which should relax me.

But I don't feel relaxed. Because he looks familiar to me. I can't make out his face beneath his hat, his pulled-up jacket collar. I can only see the hint of his profile beneath that beard. But that's

The First Time I Saw Him

enough. It's enough for me to know that I have seen him somewhere before now.

"That's him," Bailey says.

My heart starts pounding, and I force myself to take several deep breaths. I force myself to stay tucked behind that clothes rack for longer than I would like before we exit the store. I scan the street, our side of the sidewalk—the other. The man, familiar as he was, no longer in view. Which does and doesn't calm me.

We keep walking, my hand on Bailey's lower back, keeping her close. Until we turn onto Avenue Gabriel and walk halfway down the block, where we arrive at the small path to the hotel entrance, the red and black doors greeting us. I hold the door open for Bailey and we walk in.

La Réserve's lobby is small and homey, like walking into a Parisian apartment building. It's meant to feel like a Parisian apartment building; the reception area like a living room, a beautiful outdoor garden to enjoy breakfast, a library you could spend the afternoon in, brushed up against a small bar.

And then there's the staircase, winding and solitary, which takes you up to one of only forty rooms.

Forty keys, as the receptionist who showed Owen and me to our room had said. That always stuck with me. Forty keys leading to just forty beds—no other hotel in Paris quite like it. You could go days without seeing the other guests. You could feel like you have the whole place to yourself.

When we walk into the reception area, there is no room number left for us. No one in the lobby to meet us. But I know where we are going.

At least I think I do. I lead Bailey to the staircase, behind the elevators. The large and winding staircase, that will lead us to room 202.

The room where Owen and I stayed for our honeymoon. Even seeing the gold plate on the door takes me back there. I remember it well: a cozy sitting area, and a silver soaking bathtub, large steel windows peeking out at The Grand Palais. The Eiffel Tower clear and promising from the side of the small balcony.

We'll be back, Owen had said, sitting on that balcony that last morning. *This won't be the last time here.*

So it's no surprise that I'm thinking it. That Bailey turns to me and I know we are both thinking it. We are both thinking it's him, finally him.

I knock on the door. And Bailey grabs my arm.

She doesn't ask me if it's her father who is about to answer. But I know that she wants to ask. A part of her wants to know what to do if it is him. That, I want to tell her, will reveal itself. But that's not what she needs to hear.

So I lean in and tell her what she does.

"I've got you," I say. "Either way. I promise."

She nods at me, and I can feel her calm down. I can feel her find her center again, knowing mine is intact.

Why is mine intact? Especially at a moment where it would have every reason not to be. Maybe it's that I know enough to know that Owen wouldn't send us all this way unless it was to get to him. Or, at the very least, someone we love.

And I'm not wrong. Not about that part.

But when the door opens, it's not Owen standing there.

It's Nicholas.

Part II

Good luck to you, even so. Farewell!
But if you only knew, down deep, what pains
are fated to fill your cup before you reach that shore,
you'd stay right here . . .

—Homer

Part II

Five Years Earlier

In New Zealand, He Learns Patience

During Owen's first year in New Zealand, there was an unexpected cold snap. In Marlborough, winemakers get used to cooler temperatures—they ready themselves for the grapes to take longer to ripen—but this was something else. This cold snap came on fast and quick and didn't dissipate. The grapes not ripening, frost sticking to the vines. The worst harvest they'd had in years.

The harvest, Owen's first, nearly ruined.

He didn't leave Marlborough for that whole harvest. He spent his days in the vineyard helping to salvage what could be salvaged. He worked the vines until his skin blistered from the cold and his fingers were calloused and until he was too exhausted to think.

Then he stayed up all night thinking, the same questions working their way through his head: How was he going to get Hannah and Bailey out of the mess he was responsible for? How was he going to ensure they were safe?

These weren't theoretical questions. These were the only questions.

It might seem random that he ended up in New Zealand—that maybe he was just trying to get as far away as he could. But it wasn't random.

Owen and his mother had lived in Las Cruces, New Mexico, when Owen was a baby—back when his mother was still hoping his father would want to spend time with him—back when she thought that he would come to deserve being a father.

By the time he was two (by the time Owen remembered anything), his mother had given up and had relocated the two of them to Texas. Fredericksburg, Texas—the heart of Texas wine country, lush and historic, and eighty miles outside of Austin.

Shortly after they first moved there, Owen's mother became friends with a local vintner named Tom. From what Owen remembered about him, he was tall and wiry with a thick mustache. And he was kind. That was the primary thing that Owen remembered. Tom was always nice to Owen, and always so nice to his mother. Which, even as a young boy, he knew was new to her in a way it shouldn't have been.

Tom wasn't a huge part of their daily life. His mother didn't have time for a man to be a huge part of anything. Her primary focus was Owen. Owen always felt that focus in what his mother said, and in what she did. In everything about how she lived her life. She got a job as an assistant teacher at his local elementary school. So her hours matched Owen's. She supplemented her pay by waiting tables at a bar near UT-Austin on the weekend.

She'd leave Owen in the John M. Kuehne Physics Mathematics Astronomy (PMA) Library during her afternoon shifts. She made friends with the research librarian, who kept an eye on Owen. Owen would sit at a table quietly, drinking an apple juice and working on his math homework and the supplemental math workbooks his mother managed to afford for him. He loved math. It wasn't a punishment for him, spending his afternoons this way. It was a victory.

But even with both of his mother's jobs, they couldn't afford a lot of extras. Certainly, his mother didn't seem to treat herself to a lot.

Maybe this is why it was notable to Owen—and probably why he remembered—that his mother would get a case of wine after every harvest from a small-batch biodynamic vineyard in Marlborough.

The First Time I Saw Him

Billow Lake Private Select Wines. A beautiful old barn on the label, a vineyard laid out behind it. A single bottle of their highly rated pinot noir retailing for upward of 280 NZD.

Owen never asked his mother how they could afford such nice wine. He didn't want her to misunderstand and feel guilty—especially not when he was glad that she was treating herself to anything. But she volunteered it at some point. She volunteered that the wine was a present from the label's winemaker: *Do you remember my friend who used to live nearby? He moved to New Zealand. Do you remember my friend Tom?*

The way she said *friend* was like something he never heard coming out of his mother's mouth, like a prayer.

More than three decades later, Owen opened the door to Billow Lake Wines' tasting room.

It was in that old barn. The barn had since been renovated—and was large and clean. There was a long bar for the tastings, a series of two-tops scattered throughout. There was a young guy wiping down the bar top in a flannel shirt and jeans.

He looked up and smiled in Owen's direction.

"I'm sorry, bro . . ." he said, his accent thick and warm and friendly. "Tastings are done for the day."

That was when Tom walked out from the backroom, carrying a box of wine. He saw Owen standing there, and he did a double take. That double take alone brought a strange comfort to Owen—the only real comfort to Owen that he'd had since leaving Bailey. Since leaving Hannah.

"Hey, there," Tom said to him.

Owen nodded in his direction. "Hello."

The bartender looked back and forth between them, confused, Tom quickly motioned in Owen's direction, figuring out a way to turn whatever weirdness the bartender might have felt in the room, moving around in the air.

"Go ahead and introduce yourself to Simon . . ." he said to Owen. "We're not formal around here."

Owen thought of the name on his passport. It was an Irish passport. Lucas Timothy McQuade.

"I'm Lucas," he said. "But I go by Luke."

"Luke's going to be taking on Buckland's old position," Tom told Simon. "Set him up at the staff quarters. I'll finish up here."

"Fine, then," Simon said. "I'll just grab my stuff."

When Simon disappeared into the back room, Tom turned back to Owen.

"After you freshen up, come back here and find me. I'll take you to the vineyard, show you around."

Owen nodded. "Will do."

Then Tom looked at him one more time, up and down. His eyes blinking in double speed, his voice cracking as he started to speak.

"You look just like her, you know."

"I've been told."

This was as close as either of them came to acknowledging who Owen was. Tom took the cue from Owen introducing himself as Luke. Tom clocked what was happening in his own body, the pain he was feeling, just knowing how much trouble Owen must have been in, to need to show up there.

"I was real sorry to hear she passed," Tom said. "I'm still sorry."

It caught Owen in the chest, shutting his breath down for a moment. It didn't matter that it had been a lifetime ago—two lifetimes ago, really—since his mother had gotten sick. Since she'd been gone from him.

He had just turned eighteen, just gotten to college, hadn't even met Kate yet. But the loss of his mother could still rock him—rock

The First Time I Saw Him

the ground under him—in a way he knew he'd never completely recover from. In a way he only started to recover from the moment he laid eyes on Bailey.

He could see that Tom held that grief too. His eyes glazing over for a moment—but for just a moment—before he turned away. Before he started putting the wine bottles down on the countertop, getting back to work.

A silent agreement was made in that moment. A silent agreement was made to never speak of it beyond this conversation.

That was the only time, in five years, that they let the truth sit there between them. Not just his mother, but who Owen really was—and what it meant to him that, on the other side of the world, running for his life, there was someone who knew the thread of it. The person that Owen was trying to reclaim.

It stopped Owen from being completely anonymous.

And Owen suspected that it was its own kind of danger, being anonymous. You need someone to know you, so you don't disappear.

So you can remember too, as if Owen needed the reminder. His one job now. His only job.

Get back to them.

∼

In the mornings, Owen would be in the vineyard by 5 a.m.

He tried not to think during the day. He tried not to let himself think about Hannah and Bailey. The work helped. His hands and body busy for ten hours straight, often longer. Tom ran a biodynamic vineyard, which meant there were certain rules to the harvesting. There were certain rules to every aspect of farming—to taking care of the vineyard and the farm and the entirety of Tom's land. The rules were comforting, connective.

The more Owen learned, the more Tom allowed him to do. He helped maintain the vines and the soil and the tea gardens. He worked the compost pile and the beehive and the chicken coop.

At night, bone-tired, he'd get into the small twin bed in the staff room. Eventually, but never for long, he would sleep.

Once a week he walked to one of five nearby towns and spent the afternoon at either a coffee shop or the local library. He spent the afternoon somewhere with internet access. He knew that the organization was not tracing every worldwide search associated with Hannah Hall or Bailey Michaels or Nicholas Bell. But he operated as though they were. He used a public computer and a shrouded IP address and avoided certain key words.

And once a month, on these trips, he would let himself check on them. He wouldn't search for them directly—not in those early days, at least—but, rather, search for things related to them.

As an example: He would scan Bailey's high school's public social pages. He'd scour the public page just to catch a glimpse of Bailey in one of the school musicals. A video of her singing. Sometimes both.

It was a long time before he let himself go to Hannah's website, her Instagram feed. But he would let himself look up Jules's new photo essays in the *San Francisco Chronicle*—knowing Hannah would always leave a supportive comment. Her name there, among the others, a calming reminder that she was okay. She was, for the moment, safe.

At night, nearly every night, he would plan. No matter how tired he was, sleep never lasted for long.

The pain would rise up so fast, cutting him, a fierce pinch hitting behind the ribs. Visceral and immediate. Every fucking time. One memory, in particular, was wedged into his subconscious, apparently. It was wedged in the space between what Owen would allow himself

The First Time I Saw Him

to consciously hold on to about Hannah and what he, apparently, had no choice but to hold on to about her.

That very first moment. In her studio in New York. That very first moment they locked eyes, like a prelude to all the rest of it.

He was bent down by Hannah's desk—a large farm table—Hannah a few feet from him. It was easy to say that she was beautiful (which she was), effortlessly beautiful in a tank top and paint-splattered jeans. It was easy to admit he was in awe of her, especially surrounded by her work.

But it wasn't any of that. Or, at least, it wasn't as simple as that.

It was something that was stitched into him—in a way that nothing before had ever stitched into him.

It was what happened to him that very first moment—when Hannah turned toward him.

The first moment with his wife, and the last with her. Of course, you never know when you're having your last moment with the person you love. Owen certainly didn't know. Hannah was just walking him out to his car. She didn't do that every morning, but she did it the last morning.

They walked down the docks together and said goodbye by his car in the parking lot. She kissed him goodbye, slow and lingering. *I love you*, she said, like any other morning. *See you tonight.*

Because, of course, she counted on the fact that she would.

It felt like another injury. It was also further proof of what he had lost, what he had allowed himself to lose. A fitting punishment for what he'd had no right to reach for in the first place.

Now, it would wake him at night, like a jolt. That last moment with her, juxtaposed up against the first, playing back on an unforgiving loop.

It was just as well. He'd turn on the dingy light by his twin bed and put on a pot of coffee. He'd get back to work.

He was mapping the organization in detail. The entire family. He made charts on Frank. Detailed charts. He made charts on all six of Frank's children, knowing that they were the key to it—what Owen would need to do next.

At first, and for a long time, he tried to figure out how to do this on his own. Every mapped-out plan, every possible escape route.

There had to be a way to do it on his own, he thought. But there was always the moment that he realized he needed him to pull it off.

Isn't this how it worked? How you start is so often where you need to return. That was certainly the case here.

There was only one road. One road to help Hannah and Bailey. One road to keep them safe.

And it always led him back to Nicholas.

Thirty Years Ago

"Well, since you asked . . ." Nicholas said. "We finally met the boyfriend."

Frank perked up. Of course he did. If Frank wanted to hear anything, it was something about the kids.

"The math whiz?"

"I wouldn't say *whiz*."

"If you didn't say it, how would I know?"

They were sitting on Frank's back deck, looking out over the bay and downtown Miami. Nicholas had been there for almost two weeks now. He had gotten on a plane as soon as Frank called to tell him. Nicholas and Meredith had both gotten on a plane. Meredith was trying to help with the kids.

How do you begin to help with six children (one of whom was barely out of diapers) who suddenly, and out of nowhere, no longer had a mother?

It was the freakiest of things. Frank's wife, Jenny, had gone to visit an old friend of hers in the Florida Keys and they had taken a helicopter ride for the friend's birthday. A sunset helicopter ride where they drank champagne from plastic flutes and saw a variety of marine life—stingrays and sharks and dolphins.

That night, Jenny's leg started to swell up and she decided to turn in early. She decided to turn in early because it wasn't just her leg, but also a sharp pain in her lungs. Her friend had offered to take her to the local emergency room, but Jenny thought there was no need. She'd rather, she said, get a good night's sleep. She'd go and see her friend's doctor in the morning, if necessary.

But Jenny didn't wake up in the morning. That swelling—a blood clot—either from the helicopter or the plane ride to Florida (or both) had traveled to her lungs. And Jenny was gone. Just like that.

Frank was left without his wife. He was left only with his guilt. So much guilt that it was threatening to subsume him. Taking away his sleep, his energy, his sanity.

It had been Frank's idea, after all, that Jenny take a trip with her friend—to take a few days away from the kids, a few days for herself. The morning of the trip, Jenny had decided she didn't want to go, but Frank had insisted. *It will do you good*, he'd told her. The first lie Frank had ever told her. The words Frank kept repeating to Nicholas, like an omen and an apology in one.

Nicholas refilled Frank's glass of whiskey, tried to keep the conversation on the lighter side, to keep it away from work. Work was a mess, which was another problem. There were defections and anger and a big trial coming up. Nothing Frank wanted to be reminded of, nothing that he needed to be reminded of.

You never need a reminder when everyone is gunning for you, just like Nicholas didn't need a reminder that his hands were in too much of it.

It was something Nicholas had planned to discuss with Frank, getting his hands out of so much of it. Nicholas planned on starting the discussion of paring his involvement all the way back.

But now there was this.

For now, only this.

"What's the boyfriend's name again?" Frank asked.

"Ethan."

The First Time I Saw Him

"And why don't you like him?"

"I like him fine. I didn't say I didn't like him."

"Nick, come on . . ."

"No, I just think Kate's awfully young to like him so much. They both are so young. What's the rush? And Meredith is no help. She loves him. It's like they're already planning the wedding . . ."

Frank smiled at him, his first smile in days, it seemed. Then he reached over and patted Nicholas's arm.

"Get on board, friend. You don't get a vote."

"What do I get?"

"To keep your mouth closed and welcome him into your home with open fucking arms. Isn't that what Meredith always says? I feel like I've heard her say that. That's what Jenny always says."

Then, hearing himself, Frank stopped smiling.

"Said. That's what Jenny always said."

Nicholas turned to his friend.

"I don't know how to do this without her, Nick," he said.

"I know."

"I don't know how to do this just me . . ."

"Well, good thing it isn't just you then."

Nicholas put his hand on Frank's shoulder. And Frank started to cry.

The Big Island

Let's talk it through.

There were only a handful of times when Owen had left New Zealand in the last five years. Six times, to be exact.

Each time that he left, he knew, was more dangerous than the time before it.

But that was the only choice. To fix this, he needed to move closer and closer to the problem.

The first time, he only had to mail a letter. He flew to Fiji to send a letter to Nicholas at The Sanctuary, Nicholas's lake house in Texas Hill Country.

He couldn't simply email Nicholas. He knew they would be checking Nicholas's email. Forever now. Owen also didn't doubt that Nicholas would be all too eager to turn Owen in, even if his email got past them.

That left him limited choices. And he couldn't risk the postmark being from New Zealand. He didn't even want the postmark to be from Australia. So he flew sixteen hundred miles just to mail that letter.

He put it on specific stationery—that first letter. He used the stationery from a hotel in Hawaii. Nicholas's favorite hotel on the Big Island in Hawaii. Owen had downloaded the stationery from their website.

Owen chose to use that stationery so that Nicholas would know, beyond a doubt, that the letter was from him. Even though Owen didn't sign it. Even though, of course, he couldn't sign it.

If something happens to you, they'll be in danger, he wrote. *You know this is true. I'll be in touch . . .*

The second time Owen left New Zealand was six months later, the night before Bailey graduated from high school. He didn't intend to fly back to San Francisco, not at the start of this. One could argue that there was no excuse for him flying so close to where Hannah and Bailey were unless (subconsciously, for just a moment) he needed to again be near where they were. Unless, and he was conscious of this part, he couldn't stand to miss Bailey's graduation entirely. What she had been working for, who she was becoming.

But he knew there was another reason as well. He was starting to test the waters. For this plan to work, he needed to be in and out of America. He wasn't worried about himself. He was worried about Hannah and Bailey. He needed to see what he could get away with while Nicholas was still around to help protect them.

Owen also knew there was no room for error. No room for the note to be intercepted or disregarded.

No. This needed to be a hand delivery. He flew to San Francisco and took a car service straight to the Hotel Drisco, where Nicholas was staying. It wasn't a surprise that Nicholas was staying there. Bailey's graduation was being held a few miles away at Kezar Stadium. And Hannah always liked to have her out-of-town guests stay at the Hotel Drisco, a beautiful boutique hotel in Pacific Heights that housed Hannah's wood-turned bowls and furnishings in nearly every suite.

On the car ride into San Francisco proper, Owen hacked into the hotel's system and figured out which room Nicholas was staying in. He took the elevator up to his floor and waited. He waited until housekeeping came to clean—the ROOM BEING SERVICED sign hanging from the doorknob—the door slightly ajar.

He walked in and said he forgot something and left the manila envelope faceup in Nicholas's suitcase—where he could be sure that Nicholas would find it. He included a lot of things in that envelope—a lot of data points about the organization that Nicholas couldn't ignore, about their leadership, about Frank himself.

Then Owen signed it with a simple invitation. As though anything between Nicholas and him got to be simple.

If you tell me where to meet you, I'll be there.

After, Owen walked out of the airport and back into the waiting car. The car, which drove him a few minutes out of the way to Kezar Stadium. He couldn't see anything from the road—certainly not his daughter. But the parking lot was full, and he knew she was inside, beginning the next step in her life.

On the plane he let himself imagine it. Nicholas coming back to the hotel that night—proud and happy and a little bit weary—to find the note there. Would he throw it out? Would the emotion of the day propel him, despite himself, to put it back in the suitcase to consider for later?

Because he knew that at this point, Nicholas would have to respond. For this to work he would have to respond.

Then, six months later, Nicholas did respond. Six months and two weeks later, to be exact. Owen didn't know what changed in those six months, but he knew something must have changed for Nicholas to decide it was time to engage.

On his weekly visit to a local library (this week into Picton), Owen saw that he engaged. Nicholas was in Hawaii, staying at that hotel where he loved to take the family for the holidays. The hotel on the Big Island where Nicholas used to take Kate and Charlie growing up every Christmas, and where Charlie's kids spent Christmas too, until Nicholas went to prison. Where, in the last few years, he had taken Hannah and Bailey too.

The hotel whose stationery Owen used to mail that first letter.

Bailey shared a photograph on her Instagram grid of the whole family celebrating Christmas Eve. Charlie and his ex-wife (who tried to spend holidays together for the kids) and the twins and Bailey (home for her first Christmas break from school) and Hannah. Of course, Hannah.

Caption reading: *Another Day in Paradise*

Here was the important part. In the photograph, the family was sitting around a beachside firepit. They were making s'mores and sharing frozen hot chocolate and laughing, all of them laughing together.

Charlie and Hannah and Bailey and the cousins. And flanked by the twins and by Bailey—flanked by all of his grandchildren, all in one place together, like a miracle—was Nicholas.

Owen knew that Nicholas didn't let himself be photographed often, and never on social media. So Owen could imagine the rest of it: Nicholas telling Bailey that it was okay to post it. Bailey not knowing why of course.

That this was a message to Owen.

It was a message for him.

Owen walked out of the library and headed down to Queen Charlotte Sound and rented a room at a small bed-and-breakfast. He paid cash for a flowery corner room that cost him a week's wages.

Then he got a fresh burner phone and scrambled the connection. He scrambled the connection and called that hotel in Kona.

It was after midnight in Kona when he called, but Owen had no time to waste. It was two days after Christmas—two days since Bailey posted the photograph.

He knew it was possible that Nicholas had already checked out and was on his way home to Austin. Calling Nicholas on a phone that the FBI and the organization would be tracing was a risk Owen couldn't take.

When the receptionist answered, Owen thought his fear was confirmed—that Nicholas had already left. Because when he asked for Nicholas Bell's room, the receptionist responded that there was no guest at the hotel with that name.

But then Owen remembered. Nicholas never checked into a hotel under his own name. Shortly after he started working with the organization, he changed Kate and Charlie's surname from Bell to Smith. It was just a precaution then. But as Nicholas's job got riskier, he took other measures to distance himself from his family—to separate out his work life from his home life. To separate out any of the dangers of his work life, touching anyone he loved. Owen knew this. He knew that Nicholas did what he could do to keep his family safe. It was, of course, not enough.

"Would you connect me with Meredith Smith's room, please?" Owen said.

"I do see we have a Meredith Smith staying with us . . ." the receptionist said. "One moment, sir. I'll transfer you."

"Hello," Nicholas said, picking up after the first ring.

He was awake and ready for the call. Because it had been a message for Owen. A message or a trap.

"Thank you," Owen said. "For picking up."

Nicholas didn't respond, not at first. He stayed quiet.

If this was a trap, Nicholas could be slow timing this call. Despite the scrambler, despite any precautions, Nicholas could be tracing him to this small bed-and-breakfast on Queen Charlotte Sound—twenty-four miles from the vineyard where Owen slept every night, twenty-four miles down that stunning and too-short winding road.

If Nicholas was tracing him, he would be tracking Owen's location to a manageable field. He could send men—the organization could send men—to every house and farm and vineyard in the area. There weren't many. They would find Owen.

Owen held the line anyway. He held the line and he waited.

Finally, Nicholas cleared his throat. And he spoke.

"Turns out I love her more than I hate you," he said. "Both of them. Bailey and Hannah . . ."

That didn't sound like Nicholas, at least the Nicholas that Owen had once known. Except maybe it did now. Owen wouldn't know, really, what Nicholas sounded like now. Who he even chose to be now. But he had to imagine that it had softened Nicholas: getting to spend these last several years with Bailey, his granddaughter, who was so much like her mother. Her face and her skin and her spirit. Nicholas getting to know Hannah too—Hannah who it was impossible (in Owen's biased view) not to fall in love with.

The time Nicholas had been granted with both of them probably helped Nicholas make room for it—if not between Owen and Nicholas, certainly within Nicholas himself. A kind of thawing.

"I assume we need to do this in person?" Nicholas said.

"Yes," Owen said. "And you'll need to bring everything."

"I don't need you to tell me that."

And then—like a promise, or a warning shot—Nicholas gave the instructions for what would happen next.

It would involve a trip back to the hotel in Hawaii in two months' time. Nicholas provided a date in February for them to

The First Time I Saw Him

meet there. An instruction for Owen to rent room 1807. And only room 1807.

"Anything else?" Nicholas asked.

But, before Owen even answered, Nicholas had already hung up.

∼

The road into the Big Island hotel was lined with royal poinciana trees. Coconut palm trees. The front drive framed by monkeypods.

There was no denying it was beautiful: the rolling hills and the small bungalows blending into the landscape, ocean as bright and blue here as he'd ever seen. In all the years that he and Kate had been together, they'd never visited the island. She was too busy studying for the LSATs. Running the law review.

Then, Kate was out of law school and starting her law career: starting it off fiercely as a clerk for a Texas Supreme Court judge—Kate giving every ounce of energy to that incredible job, to being a young mother.

She used to talk about the Big Island with an intense love though. Kate loved reliving the memories of spending time on this island with her family growing up—the feel of that tropical air, days wading through that ocean together. The sense of calm she felt walking through the hotel lobby for the first time (every time) and taking a first sip of their welcome drink: a secret blend of local rum and fresh mangos and guava juice. (Minus the rum when she was a child.) *Can't wait for you to try it*, she'd say.

It was one of many reasons why Owen turned down the drink now, his heart turning in on itself at the memory. Kate's smile, Bailey's smile.

He signed his paperwork and nodded politely when a staff member insisted on showing him the property (the koi pool and the firepits and the hammocks dotting the great lawn) before taking him to his room—finally taking him to his room—on the second floor of one of those small oceanfront bungalows.

When Owen was alone, he locked the dead bolt and waited until he was certain the staff member wasn't coming back. Then he closed the shades and put the DO NOT DISTURB light on and walked over to the door that connected to Nicholas's suite.

He unlocked his side of the door and he knocked. And he waited. He didn't have to wait long.

He heard the click, the door unlocking from Nicholas's side.

Nicholas, suddenly, standing before him, in khaki pants and a short-sleeve button-down linen shirt.

Nicholas, standing there holding a gun. He pointed it directly at Owen's heart. The barrel touching his chest.

Fast and hard, that barrel digging into his chest.

For a second, Owen thought Nicholas was going to shoot him. For a second, Nicholas almost did shoot him. He cocked the trigger, his hand steady. Owen held his eyes. The gun against his heart, but he held Nicholas's eyes. Because this would be okay too. Because if he were dead, Hannah and Bailey would be safe. At least, they would be safer than they were now. With Owen gone, they at least couldn't one day be used as a bartering tool to get to him. But they could still be used for revenge.

Nicholas seemed to realize this at the same moment Owen did. Or, more accurately, he seemed to remember this at the same moment that Owen came to the same conclusion. That's the thing about what we don't want to know. It catches up to you whether you pretend you can avoid it or not.

Nicholas put the gun down, Owen's heart beating loudly. Beating where that gun just was.

The First Time I Saw Him

"You look like shit," Nicholas said.

"You don't look so great yourself," Owen said.

Nicholas glared at him. "I've got thirty years on you, what have you been doing that you look so bad?"

Before Owen could answer, Nicholas shook his head. "You know what? I don't fucking care."

He motioned toward the dining room table, a dozen boxes of files covering it. A dozen boxes of files (containing some twenty thousand documents and emails and correspondence). Two unopened laptop computers. Several legal pads.

"Let's get to work," he said.

Someone's Safe Harbor, Just Not His

They only left their hotel rooms at night.

They'd take a walk on the beach after most of the resort was asleep. Late-night walks, when the resort was quiet, their feet in the cool sand.

The rest of the time, they dug in. They recorded. And they tabulated. And they discussed. They ordered room service and kept the DO NOT DISTURB sign on their doors and declined housekeeping.

They compiled all of it. They organized every written piece of correspondence between Nicholas and the organization. Nicholas started at the beginning and walked Owen through the history in chronological order—what was written down, and the many things that weren't. He walked him through everything from that very first meeting with Frank on Fisher Island, nearly four decades ago, leading up to the present day.

Every case, every conversation, every piece of testimony.

There was a lot that wasn't relevant or that they couldn't use. But going through it led them to what they could.

And Nicholas walked Owen through the rest of it in great detail. He walked him through what Owen most needed to know.

The most important part of all of this: Frank's children.

There were six of them in total.

Quinn was the oldest, and Frank's favorite. She was followed by Teddy, Frank's oldest son and Quinn's Irish twin, who was not even fourteen months younger than his sister. And, at least the way Teddy saw it, always trying (and failing) to catch up—especially when it came to their father's affection.

Frank's second son, Dominic, was eighteen months sober—the longest that Dominic had ever been sober. He was working in the music industry in Franklin, Tennessee, just outside Nashville. He had three kids—two from his last marriage, a stepson from his current (and fairly new) marriage. He was married to a wonderful woman he met at rehab, even though that is advised against. Each of them doing their best so far to hold the other accountable.

Then came the twins, Sarah and Elena. They lived in Silver Lake, down the street from each other, where they hosted an extremely popular fashion podcast, more than two million Instagram followers between them. Not to mention eight kids between them—who they raised more like siblings than cousins. Sarah and her husband had three boys and a girl, Elena and her partner, Elizabeth, had three girls and a boy.

Lastly, there was the family baby, Bradley, who was freshly out of law school and an assistant district attorney in Miami. He lived five miles from his oldest two siblings but mostly kept his distance from them—tried in the ways that counted to keep his distance from all of them—because, in his mind, he had chosen the opposite life.

He hadn't yet learned, as Nicholas had, that often opposites were more closely related than anything that worked to meet in the middle.

Nicholas outlined extensive details about all the children—because Owen needed to know all of it. In terms of next steps, all of the children were important.

But for the most part, Owen and Nicholas focused on the oldest two children. Quinn and Teddy—the two that Frank was grooming to take over one day. The day, Owen thought, this would all start to be urgent.

Quinn was the apple of Frank's eye. In part because she looked exactly like her mother, even if on the inside she was the opposite.

Quinn Jennifer Campano Pointe, who was as brilliant as Teddy, was lacking in that department. She went to Stanford, where she played D1 volleyball and became interested in the law and public health. She had never been interested in the family business—until the day it became all that she was interested in.

This was in part because of what went down with her husband. And, in part, because of what went down with Owen.

Which, unfortunately, were two sides of the same thing.

Quinn's husband, Wesley, had been a trusted lieutenant in the organization—and the highest-ranking individual whom Owen's testimony had put away under RICO. At this point, nearly two decades later, Wesley had spent more of his life in jail than he'd spent outside of it.

This was the main reason Owen was so certain that they needed an insurance policy for Bailey. For Bailey and for Hannah.

Quinn was still grieving the absence of her husband. And, as Owen knew too well—Owen and Nicholas, both—grief played out in the organization as vengeance. Vengeance was where Teddy excelled.

Teddy, aka Francis Theodore Campano Pointe: tall, too-handsome, slippery. Even as a child, he idolized his father. He wanted to grow up to be just like him. Which was the quickest way to ensure that he never managed to get there.

Teddy very much wanted to be his father's favored successor. But he didn't have the brains for it, nor the instincts. So now he spent much of his time trying to prove to his father (and Quinn) that he had both. And when he failed, he leaned on being cruel. Which, more often than not, got the job done anyway. And put him back in the place he most wanted to be anyway—back in his father's good graces.

"I feel like it needs to be said . . ." Nicholas started. "Even if you do manage to pull this off, I still don't know that she'll be able to forgive you."

They were on their midnight beach walk, most of the hotel rooms dark, the oceanfront quiet and moonlit. Owen didn't need to ask who Nicholas meant. He knew that Nicholas meant Hannah.

"I'm prepared for that," Owen said.

"There is no preparing for that."

Owen didn't argue the point. How could he? He knew that Nicholas could feel it—how Owen's heartbreak lived inside his skin. That eight thousand miles hadn't cured him of it. What he had caused. What had been lost.

And still. At the end of the day, as far as Owen was concerned, the only point was this: He loved Hannah and Bailey. With everything he was. And he would do whatever he needed to do to make sure neither of them was punished for that.

"The only thing I care about is that this works," he said.

"It will work," Nicholas said.

"We can't know that yet."

Nicholas didn't respond, at first. They had an unspoken rule on these walks to give themselves a break from discussing the work—Nicholas instead filling Owen in on Hannah and Bailey, Owen clinging to every detail, to hold in his hands for later. Bailey starting to write musicals in college, Hannah moving to Los Angeles to be close to her.

But tonight was their last night together. So it was all bleeding together. The plan. Hannah, Bailey. All of it one and the same. They didn't touch on Kate though. They never touched on Kate. The pain of her loss, the unfairness, still too sharp between them.

"A few things do need to fall in line, of course . . ." Nicholas said. "Most important is you surviving what you're setting yourself up to do here . . ."

"And you knowing Frank the way you think you do," Owen added.

"Not exactly," Nicholas said. "More like the other way around."

Twenty Years Ago

"So what is this then?" Frank asked. "Your version of handing in your resignation letter?"

It was the night of Quinn's engagement party. Nicholas and Frank were at a home in West Palm Beach for a celebration toast that was nicer than most weddings. Quinn was marrying a young lawyer who was from there. Wesley was his name. He was a good kid, smart, and supportive—and tonight was the happiest Nicholas had seen Frank in a long time. Frank couldn't hide his excitement for this upcoming wedding, for how it felt to see his daughter beaming.

And, on the work front, the threats were neutralized. That's how Frank liked to put it, and most nights Nicholas didn't let himself think too much about his part in it. How Nicholas had helped those threats be neutralized. How he had stepped outside the bounds of what he thought he would do in order to provide that help.

You spend so long saying what you won't do, keeping yourself on the right side of it, the side that you decide defines you—*I won't break the law, I won't cheat, I won't lie*—that it can never cease to surprise that you crossed over.

"I need to step back, Frank," Nicholas said. "However you want to put it."

Frank paused, but only for a moment. Then he nodded.

"I understand that. And if time's what you want, Nick, you've got it," Frank said. "It's certainly due, my friend . . ."

Nicholas didn't say anything. He was a bit surprised that Frank was agreeing so easily to him stepping away from the organization—stepping away from Frank himself. Even if these last rounds of threats were neutralized (even if Nicholas had helped to neutralize them), there was no denying that the Feds were still circling. Though, of course, when it came to Frank, they always were.

Nicholas knew that his timing didn't hurt. It certainly didn't hurt that Quinn was marrying a young lawyer. A public defender—just like Nicholas had started out. Wesley was effective, deliberate, and had already expressed his desire to be involved with the organization—an idea Frank had told Nicholas he supported.

Wesley's own father had gotten in trouble with the law while he was growing up, had been indicted for insider trading. And, so, apparently Frank's work didn't scare Wesley. He was more inclined to want to step in—to be on that side of justice. Certainly, his enthusiasm was helping Frank feel covered—for the moment, at least.

Or, really, maybe it wasn't any of that. Maybe at this point Frank knew that Nicholas was too invested (that he had given too much of himself, for too long) to completely step away. Isn't that the worst part of finding yourself too deep in? The reasons don't count anymore. You can't just get out.

"I appreciate that, Frank," Nicholas says. "I'll of course get Wesley up to speed, help set him up with the team . . ."

"That's fine," Frank said. "We'll figure it out."

"Just like that?"

"What? Did you think I'd say no to you? After all this time. You should know me better than that."

"At this point," Nicholas said. "It's me that I don't know better than that."

Some Secrets Need to Stay Secrets

Before they left, Owen and Nicholas made a plan for what happened next.

They made a plan for Owen's final two trips out of New Zealand. Trip five and trip six.

The fifth trip involved Owen crisscrossing four cities (Nashville and Los Angeles and Miami and Austin) in six days. Each stop riskier than the one before.

The sixth and final trip would begin with Owen going to find Hannah—in the last possible moment before he couldn't. Then getting to Nicholas. Getting to Nicholas so they could get started on what needed to happen next.

They planned for all of this. In every machination it could possibly go. They looked for the holes, plugged them as best they could. It was crazy what they were hoping they could get away with.

They reminded themselves the final trip would just be a contingency plan—one they prayed they wouldn't have to utilize.

Then they planned it again.

And then Nicholas said one last thing. Before they left the beachfront resort behind and the ocean air behind and got on their respective planes from that tiny airport in Kona. He said one last thing so that Owen would hear it.

"This can't end with both of us getting out alive," Nicholas said. "You need to know that."

They were standing outside of the small airport in Kona. They were about to depart on two separate flights. Two flights that would take them eight thousand miles apart.

"I know," Owen said.

"And it may be both of us."

"I know that too. We're not the two I'm worried about."

"Me neither."

They held each other's gaze, as if waiting for the other to flinch.

They didn't hug. They didn't shake hands. But neither of them flinched.

This was how they said goodbye.

Part III

My dear friend, what is this our life?
A boat that swims in the sea
and all one knows for certain about it is that one day
it will capsize.

—Nietzsche

The View from the Eiffel Tower Can Make You Forget

"So this whole time," Bailey asks, "the two of you have been planning this?"

Nicholas nods. "That's fair to say."

We are in the living room of the hotel suite. I'm sitting in an antique chair, leaning in toward Bailey and Nicholas, who are sitting on the sofa across from me. The sun is going down behind them, the wind coming in through the sheer curtains, lining Bailey's bare arms with goose bumps.

Bailey moves closer to Nicholas. He wraps his arm around her, warming her. A small gesture—a gentle moment—that she thought she wouldn't have again. Her grandfather next to her, comforting her.

This moment that I thought I'd never have either: Nicholas in front of me, caring for Bailey, the joy of his presence braiding itself through the shock of it.

We've been sitting here for a long time, working through everything Nicholas needs to fill us in on—every bit of information about Owen, about what he and Nicholas have been doing. Their joint orchestration to help get us here, to get *Bailey* here, to keep her away from danger.

"The thing is," Nicholas says, looking at Bailey, "your father was convinced, we were both convinced, that when I died, my former colleagues would renege on the deal that we made to keep you both safe. We became very concerned about that. That my former clients would utilize whatever means they could . . ."

"To get to Owen," I say for him.

"Yes, exactly." Nicholas nods. "To get to Owen."

I can hear Nicholas click against it, the sound of the name Owen on his tongue. The strangeness of referring to his son-in-law as Owen Michaels and not Ethan Young—when Ethan was the name Nicholas had called him for so long. Nicholas did that with Bailey, at first, too—moving from thinking of her as Kristin (his little granddaughter, Kristin) to calling her Bailey. But he got there with Bailey. And, apparently, he spent the last several years trying to get there with Owen too.

"We needed to test his theory," Nicholas said. "So, we created murmurs that I was sick. Let my heart condition leak to see if anything piped up through the system. Let the heart surgery leak to see what would happen . . ."

"And what did happen?" I ask.

"Nothing good . . ."

I have several follow-up questions about what that means exactly. But I stay quiet, waiting for Nicholas to get there. And circling back to the central thread. The most important thread. Owen and Nicholas have been in this together. The two of them on the same side of things—as impossible as that feels. Though, of course, it shouldn't feel like such a leap. What other side would they be on? Except for Bailey's.

Which is when I see it pop in Bailey's eyes.

"Wait . . ." she says. "So does this mean that your heart condition, the surgery . . . was that all part of this too? Are you actually okay?"

The First Time I Saw Him

"No, my love. Unfortunately that is all too real."

I see Bailey deflate. I know her so well that I can feel it vibrating off her, her fear and her hope wrapping around each other. Her grandfather is sitting here with her, but he is also still on borrowed time. He will still be taken from her. He will be taken from both of us in the not-so-distant future. But not today.

"Your security started reporting that you were being followed," Nicholas says. "Both of you, actually. And we were hearing murmurs that they were eager to deploy a more extreme intervention to locate Owen."

"Extreme intervention?" I ask. "And who are they? Frank?"

He pauses and I can see that he is reluctant to give too much detail in a way that will scare Bailey.

"Frank and I have had a long, involved working relationship for several decades now," Nicholas says. "But, over the last year, Frank began the process of handing over control to his two oldest children, Quinn and Teddy, and they have their own ideas about how our situation should be handled . . ."

"What does that mean, Grandpa?" Bailey asks. "For us?"

"Quinn and Teddy knew they couldn't do anything to renege on our agreement while I was alive," Nicholas says. "Frank wouldn't stand for that. But it became clear to your father and me that Frank's children had no intention of honoring Frank's guarantee that you'd both be safe . . . at least when I was no longer here to ensure that they did."

I unlock the rest as Nicholas starts to explain: Frank had always treated Nicholas like family—that's a large part of the reason why Nicholas was able to secure our safety. But if suddenly Frank's allegiance to Nicholas didn't have to be honored (because Nicholas was no longer a factor), neither did Bailey's and my safety.

This was why Nicholas faked his death. He knew what the organization planned to do in his absence. He and Owen both knew. So they needed that to play out now—while Nicholas was still here to control the aftermath. Which meant they had to create the illusion that Nicholas was in fact gone. It was a task that involved Nicholas being "found unresponsive" at his remote lake house as opposed to in downtown Austin, with all its bureaucracy and red tape. In that remote Texas Hill Country town, there was almost none. More importantly, Nicholas knew the local coroner well. Nicholas knew that the coroner would have no compunction (had historically had no compunction) about signing a death certificate—if it properly benefited him to do so.

"So that's why you didn't give us any warning?" I ask.

"We needed you to believe I was gone. We needed my passing to play across all fronts. That was vital to this all working." Nicholas pauses. "I certainly didn't expect that the organization would choose to act so quickly. That hours after my death was announced, they would start . . ."

"Coming for us?" I say.

Nicholas nods, and meets my gaze, his eyes giving away the betrayal he feels that this happened. And a sadness there. A sadness that I can't disregard, even if I don't yet understand what's behind it.

"We did prepare for this, though," he says. "Owen prepared for this level of response."

It catches me, stopping my breath: the proximity to this danger—Bailey's proximity to it. And everything Owen has been doing—the beating heart of everything Owen has been doing—to try and mitigate it.

I knew it in my gut. It's why I felt safe enough to get on the plane—safe enough to be sitting here now. I knew that, to protect

The First Time I Saw Him

his kid, Owen looked at this from every angle. And then every angle again. But I feel it gnawing at me all the same, something pushing its way to the forefront of my mind: The man in the army jacket on the street. He was familiar in a way I can't ignore. Familiar and potentially still too close by.

"Frank is still involved in a consulting role," Nicholas says. "But, for all intents and purposes, Quinn and Teddy are now in charge of the daily operations out of Florida. And since he's stepped back, Frank doesn't spend much time there. He spends most of his time in the South of France."

"The South of France?" Bailey asks.

He nods. "In a town called Èze," he says. "About ten hours from here."

Èze. I'm familiar with it—the famous cliffside village, the beach far below it. I spark to a foggy memory of driving past the village several years ago. Pre-Owen. Pre-Bailey. I was on the way to Monaco with a client (we were doing an installation on her vacation home), and she pointed out Èze as we passed by.

It is a town trapped in time, high on its cliffside, the medieval rock stunning and jagged, even from the road far below.

"Frank turns eighty on Saturday, and he's having a party to celebrate. All six of his children will be there, his eighteen grandchildren, a few of his closest friends. He flew everyone in . . ." He pauses. "He's taking over the local hotel for the weekend. The forty-five rooms booked for his guests, the entire hotel closed for tomorrow night's party . . . I'm on the guest list, of course."

"But they think you aren't alive," Bailey says, uneasy.

"That part will be a surprise, I assume."

Nicholas offers a smile, a small uneasy laugh. My shoulders start to seize up—like a warning shot as I work through it in my head.

That's why this is all happening now. This party. This isolation. Owen and Nicholas's ability to make sure that everyone is in one place for whatever they are orchestrating. For this ambush.

"And where in your calculation will Bailey and I be?" I ask.

He turns to Bailey. "You will be in a safe location," he offers. "With your father, of course."

A safe location with Owen. The pulse gets louder in my head, even at the idea—of being with him somewhere, of being with him anywhere. What that might begin to look like. What that might begin to feel like.

"You're planning on going to Èze alone?" I ask.

"I am."

"That's totally not safe," Bailey says.

And I can hear it rising up in her, her distress at this possibility.

"Frank would never hurt me," Nicholas says.

Nicholas says this with absolute authority. But that's not the whole story. Because it's not just about Frank anymore. Frank isn't in charge, fully. Everything about what's going on now proves that. It's about Frank's children who, despite their father, apparently have no allegiance to any of us—not even to Nicholas.

"Bails . . ." I say. "Could you please give me and your grandfather a minute alone? I need a minute alone with him."

"Absolutely not."

"Bailey . . ." I say.

I turn and meet her eyes. She is holding on to every word too closely for me to process and figure out how to best protect her at the same time.

But she isn't having it. She holds my gaze, refusing to stand down, and giving me her *I'm not a kid anymore* glare. Even as she crosses her arms in a way that makes her look very much like one—the Bailey of yesteryear creeping into the room, the Bailey who argued with

The First Time I Saw Him

me, even when she agreed with me. And certainly when, like now, she didn't agree at all.

I take a deep breath, knowing I don't have time to fight this battle. I don't have time to do anything but get ready for what needs to happen next.

I turn back to Nicholas. Nicholas, who I've come to love. Nicholas, who I won't leave to hold this all alone.

"I'm going with you," I say.

"Hannah..."

"Nicholas, you just finished telling us that Frank isn't the only one making the decisions anymore. Isn't what's going on now proof of that?" I ask. "I'm not letting you do this alone."

He locks eyes with me as he figures out how to argue that point. But he isn't going to convince me, regardless of what he says. How could he begin to convince me? He can't, not when this involves my family and my husband. Not when it involves an agreement that I helped to forge between him and the organization.

I haven't gotten this far—I haven't kept Bailey safe for this long—by taking a back seat to anyone. And I don't trust anyone to negotiate on my behalf. Not Nicholas, not anyone.

And then there's the other reason—the one that involves Nicholas himself. Our last five years together slam into focus: those early trips he took to Sausalito to spend time with Bailey; her concussion and that small hospital room in Utah; college move-in day (and move-out day); all the celebrations and holiday dinners and late-night calls in between. The moments that are impossible to tally.

Isn't that how it happens? You add it all up (you can't begin to add it up) and you don't just love someone. You *know* him.

And I know it in my gut, staring back at him now. As much as Nicholas is saying that he doesn't want me there with him, a piece of him does—a piece of him that he can't seem to hide, as much as he is trying.

Which may help explain the urgent pull I feel to protect him.

"Hannah," Nicholas says. "If the plan goes sideways, you should be together, all three of you, so you can run . . ."

"That's the thing, Nicholas," I say. "I want to be with you so that the plan doesn't go sideways . . ."

Which is when there is a knock on the door, fast and sharp. Nicholas turns toward the door, Bailey looking at me, suddenly on edge. More on edge. And before I can even ask who is knocking, I hear a key turn in the lock, the door opening, and he's walking into the living area—the man in the army jacket and the hat. The thick beard. Strangely enough, a tray of coffees in his hands.

I stand up fast, instinctually moving in front of Bailey. Blocking her. Ready to protect her.

But then the man in the army jacket takes off his hat. And I see who it is. Who I didn't quite recognize beneath the hat and that beard.

Seth. Nicholas's longtime bodyguard. I've met him several times over the last five years—Bailey and I both have. He's been working with Nicholas for more than two decades now. He has stayed with Nicholas through everything, even through when Nicholas was in prison. Even, apparently, this.

Bailey steps out from behind me.

"What is going on?" she says.

Nicholas puts his hand on her arm, calming her.

"I asked Seth to keep an eye on you when you landed in LBG," he says. "A little extra security to make sure you got here safely."

"I tried to keep a safe distance," Seth says.

"You scared the shit out of us!" Bailey says. "Why didn't you just come over to us?"

The First Time I Saw Him

"I couldn't imagine a world where coming up to you wouldn't scare you more..."

Seth was right about that. Nicholas was supposed to be dead. How would it not have terrified us to suddenly have his former bodyguard tapping us on the shoulder on the streets of Paris? Before we understood the rest of it.

Seth hands us each a coffee—a most welcome cup of coffee. I wrap my hands around the cup and sit back down. Find my center again. Bailey following suit. Bailey starting to breathe again.

I should feel better with Seth there, and in some ways I do. But I know Nicholas is just going to utilize his presence as further proof that he does have this handled. That Seth will be with him in Èze. But it won't stop what's gnawing at me—my belief that if I know anything, I know that's not true.

I turn back to Nicholas. I lower my voice, calm and resolute.

"Nicholas, you and Owen aren't the only ones who spent the last five years working out an escape hatch," I say. "I need to be there."

Nicholas looks over at Bailey, who is holding on to me. "She can be stubborn, your mother."

"Believe me. I'm aware."

And maybe he expects her to argue—to insist that I shouldn't go. But if I've done anything well with Bailey, I've done this. She trusts me to know what needs to be done. For me, and for her. And she trusts me to do it.

"You can't leave me out of this, Nicholas," I say.

Nicholas nods like he understands that. Then he looks up at Seth. He looks up at Seth and then back and forth between Bailey and me.

"Unfortunately," he says. "We can't leave anyone out of this."

Sixteen Years Ago

"I can't tell you how much I appreciate it, my friend . . ." Frank said. "The sacrifice you're making to leave me out of this."

Nicholas and Frank were at an all-night diner, not too far from Nicholas's condominium in downtown Austin. It was a local favorite that served gingerbread pancakes and fresh maple syrup and decent coffee. It was, quite easily, Nicholas's favorite meal. This was mostly because it had been Kate's favorite meal growing up. The two of them often came here on Saturday mornings for breakfast, or late night on weekdays when Kate had a lot of studying to do—and she was willing to take a break and humor him.

It had been eighteen months since he lost her. Eighteen months since Nicholas was babysitting Kristin at the park, Kate walking from the courthouse to meet them. Kate had been working overtime—the justice she was clerking for writing the majority opinion on a case involving a large energy corporation. She was exhausted and in need of a weekend. They had plans to make homemade pizza that night, to watch an old Disney movie on TV, for Nicholas to put Kristin to bed—so Kate could enjoy a nightcap with her husband.

They had plans.

Then Kate was struck by a car on that walk to meet Nicholas. A car that hit her and disappeared.

She was hit by a car going fifty miles per hour on a quiet, unassuming street a handful of blocks from her home.

And all plans stopped. All plans stopped the moment Nicholas found his daughter there, on the side of the road, no longer alive.

"You don't need to thank me," Nicholas said. "It doesn't matter."

"What are you talking about?" Frank asked. "The sacrifice you're making . . . of course it matters, Nick."

"No," Nicholas said. "It doesn't. It doesn't matter anymore. Where I am."

Frank didn't argue with that, which Nicholas appreciated. There was no arguing. Grieving his daughter was who Nicholas was now—which Frank seemed to understand. Maybe because he would be the same. Or maybe it had more to do with their shared anger toward Nicholas's son-in-law, who they both blamed for this entire mess. He could hear Kate's response to this. He could hear her voice responding to everything: *That's easier, Dad, isn't it? Than blaming each other.*

But either way, since Kate died, there were only a handful of people Nicholas could stomach to be around outside his own family.

Frank was one of them. And Frank knew this, which was probably why he'd flown in for the night. He'd flown in just to have this conversation in person, this meal in person. To say his thank-you.

How do you thank someone for taking this kind of hit for you? You can't. But Frank seemed determined to try.

Nicholas was starting his sentence in forty-eight hours. The official charges stemmed from his son-in-law's testimony—from the encryption system that Ethan put together for Nicholas—from what that encryption system revealed about the organization's criminal misdeeds.

But the unofficial charges were these: Nicholas wouldn't roll. He wouldn't roll on Frank, the man that he most aided and abetted. In those early discussions, the FBI was quick to point out (as if Nicholas needed it to be pointed out) that it was ironic that the person for whom Nicholas most frequently broke the law kept his hands clean because Nicholas was keeping his mouth shut.

Nicholas wasn't going to turn on Frank—and there wasn't enough to stick to Frank without Nicholas doing so.

It didn't stop the FBI, though, from bringing down some of Frank's other associates, though mostly no one in upper management. Nicholas was able to shield most of upper management by not cooperating himself. The most notable exception was Quinn's husband, Wesley. That was the sharpest blow to Frank—the loss of his own son-in-law, the loss of his planned successor.

It was the sharpest blow to Frank besides losing Nicholas himself.

"Maybe you don't think I need to say it again, but I do. I do need to say it. What you are doing, Nic . . . I'll never forget it." Frank paused, met Nicholas's eyes. "Anything you ever need from me. Any favor. It's yours."

That stopped Nicholas cold. *Any favor.* Those words rang in his ears. Like a bargain he didn't know he was making.

Nicholas must have been wearing it on his face because Frank tilted his head, taking him in, confused.

"What's that look?" he asked.

"Why would that need to be said between us?"

"I don't know. I feel like you deserve to hear it."

Nicholas didn't like that answer, but mostly because he knew Frank was trying to make him feel better. There was nothing that made him feel better. Not anymore. It was why he didn't want Frank's gratitude, nor Frank's constant assurances that the organization had nothing to do with Kate's untimely death.

He also didn't need it. Nicholas didn't believe any of the chatter that Kate's death was a result of Nicholas's decision to pull back from the organization. He didn't pay attention to the rumors that the organization went after his daughter to keep Nicholas in line—to pull him all the way back in.

Frank didn't need to give him assurances that wasn't true because how did that even make sense? It didn't, despite Nicholas's son-in-law believing otherwise. Nicholas knew that his son-in-law was blinded by his grief—by the rage that was heating up inside him, so large and unforgiving—leading him to not see clearly. To circle the blame, put it in a box. An imaginary box.

He knew, in his gut, that Frank wasn't the guilty party here. Even his wife was certain of that. If they both weren't, Nicholas would never be sitting there. Frank wouldn't even be alive. Nicholas also knew something else. It didn't matter why Kate was gone. He would never be free now anyway.

"After I lost Jenny, you know what everyone said to me? They said it would get better. They said the grief will pass." Frank paused. "I don't think I properly thanked you for never saying something that stupid."

Nicholas looked up at him.

"It doesn't pass. You learn to live with it but it doesn't fucking pass . . ." Frank shook his head, his voice catching. "But you know what did help? The only fucking thing, really. It was when I was with you. Because I knew that you loved Jenny too. That it was hard for you too. That helped . . ."

Frank leaned across the table. He leaned closer to Nicholas.

"I watched your daughter grow up," Frank said. "I loved her, Nick. I loved her like she was mine."

The First Time I Saw Him

Nicholas cleared his throat, feeling that, feeling how deeply Frank meant that.

"I know it."

"So I'm going to tell you exactly what you told me back then," Frank said. "Do you remember?"

"I don't."

"You said stop looking for joy anymore because you're not going to find it. Look for purpose. That will get you through."

Forty-eight hours until prison. Tomorrow, he would spend the afternoon with Charlie and his family. He could see the strain between Charlie and his wife, but he'd pretend not to. For the afternoon they would all pretend. And then tomorrow night, the last night, it would be just him and Meredith.

Why couldn't he find the purpose in any of that?

Nicholas knew the answer before he finished asking himself the question. Because if he could no longer help Kate, the only other thing he could find purpose in was what mattered most to her.

Kristin. Kate's daughter. Nicholas' granddaughter.

Now, she was also taken from Nicholas. Now, she was gone too. If his son-in-law had his way, she would be kept away from Nicholas for good.

Nicholas reached for his coffee, took a long sip. He was buying time while he considered it—what Frank was offering here, what (if anything) he really wanted to ask for.

"I know what I would want that favor to be," Nicholas said.

"Is that right?"

Nicholas nodded. "If the time comes."

"Okay. And what's that?"

"Bring her back to me."

Frank didn't ask who Nicholas was talking about. He didn't have to ask. He knew that Nicholas meant Kristin.

"What about him?"

"I don't care about him. Just find her and bring her home."

"If it's the last thing I do."

The Lights Stay On in Paris

After Bailey falls asleep, I sit on the balcony of the hotel suite—the Eiffel Tower in the distance, the tree lights blinking in the park across the way, the stars and moon bright in the night sky. Couples are still out enjoying the night. Couples walking hand in hand down this small street. Even at 2 a.m. At three.

Nicholas and I stayed up long after Bailey went to bed. We went through what I needed to know about the plans for tomorrow, working through it together. We worked through the entirety of the plan for the party: what he and I would be doing there, what it all would look like. Where Owen would be.

Now Nicholas is asleep too, and I keep myself awake—awake and focused—with a pot of fresh coffee beside me. I go over everything we discussed, trying to keep my emotions about it in check as I stare down at my laptop, Owen's flash drive files open on the screen, that marine compass staring back at me.

The compass takes me back to it, to my very first sailing lesson. My instructor at the academy handed me a marine compass, which looks eerily similar to this one, and he told me that it was the most important piece of equipment I needed. It was the most important because it was the most reliable.

He explained it simply: how it has a permanently magnetized needle that always points north, irrespective of a boat's position. When the boat turns, the compass continues to point at magnetic north, and the course is shown in reference to that line. That was most of my first lesson: how the compass is the one piece of navigational equipment that will operate when everything else you think you know fails.

True north, holding, even when everything else is unsteady.

When everything is shifting away from what you can control.

I roll the mouse over the compass, hold it over true north, like it's going to open a secret file that Owen wants me to find there. Like it's going to unlock everything I need to do now—to steady the ship again.

After all, isn't everything shifting away from what I thought was steady? Nicholas is alive and has been working in tandem with Owen for years now. Owen, who has been risking everything to find his way back to us.

Everything I knew has certainly shifted—but, in the many ways that matter, it's shifted only closer.

It is far closer to what I've always believed about who I married.

"You're still awake?"

I turn to see Nicholas, standing by the balcony door. He is standing there in his pajamas and a pair of the hotel's slippers. Something about looking down at them nearly does me in. Maybe because they look so soft and fluffy and inviting. All of which is in direct opposition to what we are doing here.

"Did you get any sleep at all?" Nicholas asks.

"Did you?"

He smiles and moves out onto the balcony, sitting down across from me at the small table.

"Maybe I'll sleep when this is finished," I say.

I move my laptop out of the way and refill my mug of coffee. Then I pour Nicholas a mug of coffee too. I give him a minute to take a sip, to ground himself a bit.

The First Time I Saw Him

"You look worried," he says.

"I just keep going over it in my mind," I say. "And I think we're missing something here. I do."

"In terms of what?"

"Tomorrow night. All the ways it could potentially go wrong. All the ways this could all go wrong before it's finally over."

"Not to beat a dead horse, but if you'd let me do this on my own, it could be over for you now . . ."

"That's not how this works, Nicholas," I say. "It's only over for me when it's over for all of us."

He offers a small laugh, amused by this apparently, amused or touched. "Well, if that's your criteria . . ." he says.

But he doesn't waver. Maybe because he is secure in this plan in a way I want to be able to hold in my hands too. Except I can't—not when there is something that still isn't adding up for me.

"I'm just having trouble believing it," I say.

"Which part?"

"Why, after what we are about to do here, would they ever agree to just leave us alone?"

"For the same reason that anyone agrees to anything," he says. "They don't have another option."

"Aren't you the first to say there's always another option?" I ask.

"I can be wrong sometimes."

"Not the moment I want to hear that."

"What do you want to hear, Hannah?"

I look over at my laptop, that marine compass staring back at me. I know what I'm doing. I know how to keep myself safe—and I know how to keep Bailey safe. But it's not just on me to do that, not this time. And I can't shake the feeling that we are risking something I don't want risked.

"Are you sure that Owen knows what he's doing here?" I say. "That you both do?"

"If I believe anything, it's that," Nicholas says.

Then he pauses.

"But there is something else you need to know that your husband understood a long time before I did . . ." he says.

"What's that?"

"It's hard for me to admit this," Nicholas says. "Which is why I haven't told you before now . . ."

He meets my eyes with his kind gaze. His loving gaze. This is the man who five years ago was on the other side of all this from me—and who now feels like my closest family. The person I most trust to help me do it now—get me back to my own true north. To get us all back there.

"So then," I say, "admit it quickly."

The Provençal Market Doesn't Take a Day Off

Owen moves quickly.

In the city center of Antibes, he pulls into an indoor parking lot.

It's early, not yet 6 a.m. The sun isn't quite up, the world quiet. In a few hours, this lot will be full of locals, eager to visit the businesses lining these streets: clothing stores and barbershops, brasseries. Tourists eager to see the Sacred Heart Church, the Casino Cinéma. The Théâtre Le Tribunal.

But now, it's just Owen. He looks behind him in the rearview mirror, no one pulling in or out of this parking lot. Not at 5:42 in the morning.

He weaves his way to the second floor and parks in a corner spot, turning off the ignition. Popping the trunk. His bike is waiting inside, the helmet attached to it. He pulls them out and closes the trunk, leaving the key under the passenger-side mat.

Then he puts on that helmet and bikes out to the street below—steering down the narrow roads leading through the city center and out toward Old Town—the roads getting windier as he hits the countryside and their precipitous peaks, moving him closer to the ocean, moving him past the seaside apartments.

In these early hours, most of the lights are off. A few people are up brewing their morning coffee, the blue lights of their televisions shining with the morning talk shows, cartoons for the kids.

But mostly everyone is still asleep. Owen didn't sleep. He didn't even try. He feels better on the bike, better with movement. His heart thumping, and his chest blowing out.

He pulls to the side of the road to check his phone. But he has no new voice messages waiting for him. He has no new text messages either. He isn't supposed to hear from Nicholas, not yet. But that doesn't comfort him. Nothing, at the moment, feels comforting.

In all of his planning, he didn't anticipate this—just how strange it would be, how difficult these last hours would feel. The possibility of being with Hannah and Bailey so close, and yet somehow further away.

It reminds him of that article in *Scientific American* that Hannah showed him years ago—the article that stuck with him. There was a group of scientists who studied thousands of commuters who missed their trains by five minutes, thousands of others who missed theirs by many hours.

The commuters who just missed the train had a harder time recovering from the missed departure. They spent days afterward, trying to figure out where they went wrong—what they could have shifted in their day to make up the few minutes that would have gotten them to the train sooner. The unnecessary stop for coffee, or the last-answered email that should have waited until they were on board. Anything and everything they should have skipped, so they'd have gotten there in time.

Either way, you missed it. But almost making it was so much worse.

How can Owen explain it? He's waited five years, ten months, and twenty-six days. But these last hours are all like that. Whenever he stops moving, it's like he is watching the train pull out of the station. Without him.

It's not getting him anywhere, giving too much time to that kind of worry, so he tries to move through it—the way he has spent the last nearly six years moving through it.

The First Time I Saw Him

He kicks his bike brakes, heads back into traffic, speeding up as he gets closer to Old Town Antibes, the tourist destination quiet in the morning light: the empty cobblestone streets and mostly closed restaurants, the stunning museum on the hill.

And the Provençal market, Old Town's famous market, the only place with any action at this time of day. Farmers are starting to set up their stands, early morning workers opening the marketplace.

He pulls over in front of a small coffee shop, a barista just opening the doors. He could use a cup of coffee. He could use three. But before he even walks inside—his hand on the door—he hears a voice behind him.

"*Bonjour.*"

He turns around, half-expecting to see an officer in uniform there. An officer or a security guard. Someone wanting to see his papers. Someone wanting to know more about where he has come from, why he is sweating from his early morning bike ride. Someone waiting for an explanation as to where he is going.

Owen has the answers ready for them—he's run this play several times now—and knows exactly how to make sure they don't follow him any farther than here. But it's nerve-wracking all the same.

Isn't this how it happens? You can see the whole chessboard. You organize your life to see it. But you still miss it, the smallest of missteps. The only way you lose.

But the young man behind him is not an officer. He's also not alone, a young woman on his arm, still dressed up from the night before. He is in a shiny blue suit, she is dressed in stiletto heels and a short dress—both of them looking tired and happy. And they're staring out at Owen with matching smiles.

"*S'il vous plaît, voudriez-vous prendre une photo?*"

A photograph. They want Owen to take their photograph. They're just a young couple, hoping to capture this moment for themselves. The end of a long night (an all-nighter) in the South of France.

But the young guy is looking a little sweaty and anxious as he hands Owen his cell phone, cupping his jacket pocket. Which makes Owen wonder if he wants to capture a photograph not just because it's the end of a special night—but also because it's the beginning of a special day for him too. The beginning of the day he proposes. The beginning of something new.

"*Bien sûr, je le ferai,*" Owen says.

Of course he will. Owen takes a series of quick photographs for them, the couple posing together. Happy and laughing. Then Owen hands the guy back his phone, offering him a small nod, wishing him luck.

The young guy nods back, which Owen decides to take as the guy wishing him the same. He'll take it. Because he needs it. They all do today.

They need every bit of luck they can get.

Owen walks aways from the coffee shop, deciding against going inside. Deciding against stopping anywhere else.

He gets back on his bike and keeps going. The only way he can.

Toward Port Vauban.

Toward the boat.

If You Should Lose Your Way . . .

We are driving at a steady clip down the A8 Autoroute, Paris now far in the rearview, the highway pointing us toward Èze. The highway pointing us toward Èze and an eightieth birthday party, where all of this gets decided.

Seth drives. I'm in the passenger seat beside him. Bailey and Nicholas are sitting together in the back. Bailey leans against the windowpane, taking in the scenery flashing by in the early morning light. Nicholas sitting beside her, taking in Bailey. He seems so happy, even now—even with where we are headed—just to be there beside her.

I've pulled out my laptop, and I'm working through all the charts I've made. I've mapped out everyone in the organization—everyone in Frank's inner circle, centering around the most important people in his orbit. His family. All of them will be in attendance tonight. Frank and all six of his children, all eighteen of his beloved grandchildren. They're each important to understand, in one way or another, but none more so than Frank's successors: Teddy and Quinn.

Quinn, who I keep circling back to, even now.

Quinn, who to me, feels like the key to all this, should we need it. A different lock to turn.

I scroll through to my photographs of her. She is six feet tall and blond and beautiful. She was an all-American volleyball player, who could have gone to the Olympics. But she is, instead, the heir apparent to a crime family. It was a switch that came on quickly—after Owen's testimony put her husband in prison.

Quinn and Wesley were still newly married when he started serving his sentence. Newly married with twin twenty-two-month-old boys. Boys who are close to Bailey's age now. Boys who grew up without their father. Boys who—certainly in Quinn's estimation—grew up without their father because of Owen.

This is the nexus of so much of Quinn's anger—her husband taken from her, her children's father taken from them, because Owen turned state's evidence. Of course, it was Wesley's own decisions that ultimately landed him in prison—his decisions, his multitude of crimes. But Quinn didn't want to look at that. Why would she want to look at that part? It would demand that she lean into empathy when anger was so much easier.

I turn around to face Nicholas. He is avoiding my eyes, trying to enjoy his time with Bailey.

"When is Quinn's husband supposed to get out of prison?" I ask him.

"Wesley? No time soon."

"What does that mean?"

"Well, it looked like he was going to be released after his last parole hearing," Nicholas says. "It was his first real shot at it, and Quinn made a big push. She activated everyone she could. They had a letter from the new warden about the good he's been doing inside. They had a letter from the governor. They made a hard push to get him out of there. But the parole board voted against him all the same. Three to two."

"How recently was this?"

"Two months ago. Next hearing is two years out."

Two months ago, and now at least two more years to go. That

The First Time I Saw Him

was a fresh bruise for Quinn. It would help explain why she moved so quickly to punish Owen the first moment she felt like she had an opportunity to do it. It explained why she was so willing to punish anyone close to Owen. Everyone close to Quinn's husband had been punished—with no end to his absence in sight.

"We've considered it, Hannah," he says. "Many times. We've considered the Quinn of it all."

I nod. Because I know that he thinks he has. Owen and Nicholas both think they've considered the Quinn of it all, as he is saying. But this is why I keep coming back to Quinn. Because every time I look at Bailey in the rearview, I know what I would do. I know what I'm still doing for her.

And I know that Nicholas and Owen didn't consider that part of this equation—because they can't.

You can't begin to properly consider it. It's impossible to consider the lengths a woman will go if she thinks she's protecting her family.

∼

Shortly before 3 p.m., we pull off A8 at exit 44. The exit for Antibes.

We pull into the turnaround in Old Antibes—the historical district stretched out before us; the stores and restaurants busy with the afternoon crowds, the farmers' market shutting down for the day; and a tall castle visible from its perch on the top of the hill.

A tall and quite beautiful old castle—hundreds of years old—that is now the home to Musée Picasso.

Bailey's destination.

I turn around to face Bailey. I want to go over it with her again, everything that is going to happen now. But Bailey is looking out the window and taking in the museum, readying herself. She pulls her hair back, putting her messenger bag over her shoulder. Seth is out of the car already. He is waiting for her.

She turns toward me. "Seth won't get too close?" she asks.

"Not unless you need him to."

"I won't need him to."

"I know you won't," I say. Because I feel sure of that. I feel entirely sure of that, or I wouldn't be letting her out of the car.

And still to be apart. To be apart from her when everything in my body wants to keep her near.

"Do you have any other questions?" I ask.

"Since five minutes ago?" Bailey asks. "No. I think I'm good."

But she says it with a smile, as if convincing me she's got this.

She watches for my reaction, eager to leave the car—asking, in a way, for my permission to do so. But then I feel her energy shift as she turns toward her grandfather.

She leans in to hug Nicholas goodbye, moving herself into the crook beneath his shoulder. Maybe it's the whiplash of thinking she had lost him for good. But she doesn't let go of that embrace, breathing into it, breathing into him longer than she should, her eyes getting red and foggy.

"Please be careful," she says.

"That's my line for you, kid," he says.

Then he pulls back. She holds on to him for so long that he's the one who pulls back from her.

I watch as he does. And I can see the way he starts holding his hands against his thighs, grasping his palms together a little too tightly—as if to stop himself from reaching for her again. Reaching for her and not letting go. He fights it though because he doesn't want Bailey to see how much this goodbye is hurting him.

I get out of the car and Bailey follows suit. Her bag is on her

The First Time I Saw Him

shoulder, her eyes holding on mine. I force a smile and meet her gaze, so I can give her the reminder—so I can give us both the reminder—that it's safer for her out of the car than in it.

It's safer for her away from me and what I need to do here. For all of us.

I lean in to give her a quick hug—to give her that strength.

"You've got this . . ." I say.

I leave out the part I'm sure she hears. *You've got this, even without me.*

Then I let her go.

The Sirens Have a Story to Tell

Bailey walks toward the museum.

Seth follows several feet behind her.

She doesn't turn around, but she knows he is behind her. She knows he is following her in case she needs him.

She fights against her desire to turn around. She fights the desire to see the car pulling away, moving down the cobblestone streets. To see her grandfather, again. Ever since he's been sick, she feels their goodbyes differently—the aftermath of each one, stinging.

Should she be surprised that with what's going on, she's not also focused on Hannah? That she's not worried about her? She isn't. If Bailey trusts anything, she trusts Hannah to do what is needed to take care of herself—and to take care of her.

Maybe that's what happens when you have a mother who never asks you: *What do we do now?*

You believe her that she knows.

Bailey takes a deep breath and keeps going. She walks the narrow cobblestone streets, passing the restaurants gearing up for late-afternoon cocktails and bites. The marina lit up in the distance.

She keeps going up the steep and windy hill that lands her by that former castle, a large photograph of Picasso gracing the outside. MUSÉE PICASSO, ANTIBES in large letters alongside his face.

Inside, she heads directly to the ticket booth. It's crowded. They needed it to be crowded. They needed a public place where Bailey can blend into the crowd—where they both can—so he can make sure no one followed them here. So her father can make sure they're free to do it. To go where they need to go next.

The tour guide is waiting there, just like Nicholas said he would be, holding a sign that says THE FRENCH WAY TOURS.

"Bonjour," he says. "Are you here for the four p.m. tour?"

Bailey nods. Yes, she is. The 4 p.m. tour. The last tour of the day.

The tour guide smiles and motions for her to stand with the group assembling around him. Eight to ten of them waiting for him to start walking them through.

That is all that is apparently required. She was ready to hand him her confirmed ticket. But he doesn't ask. He doesn't ask for her passport either. He doesn't need any further proof that she is on his list.

She stands to the side with the others who are waiting. A young family, two older couples, and a guy close to Bailey's age in wire-rim glasses, a backpack slung over his arm. He nods in her direction, like an acknowledgment of their shared twentysomething status. Bailey nods back, turns away.

A few moments later, the tour starts. The guide begins by sharing the history of the museum—the castle that was once the Château Grimaldi built upon the foundations of the ancient town of Antipolis. It had served as the residence for the local governor for centuries, had been a town hall, a barracks, and the Grimaldi Museum. And, for a period of time, it became the home to Picasso.

Bailey forces herself to focus, to look interested. In another world, she would be interested. But now she grows increasingly anxious as the guide walks the group through the new collection on the first floor. The visiting collection. It's a young artist's collection, paintings with lots of geometric shapes. A large triangular sculpture in the middle. The guide is explaining the artist's intention with that

The First Time I Saw Him

triangle, but Bailey only hears every third word. Her heart is racing so loudly that she thinks the rest of the group must hear it, but they don't notice.

When they get upstairs, the guide starts to move them through the Picasso Collection. He walks to the room in the back with Picasso's gorgeous plates and the painting Bailey is supposed to be looking for. The *Ulysses and sirens* painting. The bench in front of it.

He talks about the surrealist qualities—Picasso's lessons on temptation—but Bailey isn't listening. She is only listening for the moment when he motions toward the door. Toward where the group is going next.

"This way please . . ." he says.

But Bailey doesn't go with the rest of the group. She hangs back. She hangs back until after the tour group leaves. She pretends to be enamored by those gorgeous ceramic plates lining the wall. She studies each one of them for several minutes, as if someone is going to test her on them. As if someone is watching her.

Because someone is.

The young guy. The one with the wire-rim glasses. He stays back too, and he is watching her. There is no question he is watching her—the only question is why.

It could be that he is just interested in her. He's a backpacker close to her age. Maybe he is looking for someone to hang with that day, looking for someone to travel with.

Or is it something else?

She isn't waiting to find out. She pretends to be looking at a painting, Wire Rims not coming any closer. Not yet.

Then, she moves. She passes the elevator, heads toward the back steps. She flies down those steps, not looking behind her. She doesn't go back out to the street to find Seth, not yet. Not when it will disrupt the plan, the only plan that gets her to her father.

She passes by the women's room, where he might think to wait for her—if he is waiting for her. And she rounds the corner to the family bathroom, the single stall, where she locks the door behind her. She rests against the door, willing her heartbeat to slow. She rests against the door even when a few people try the lock, giving a couple of friendly knocks—before giving up, moving on.

She stays there long enough that if Wire Rims was just trying to approach her for innocent reasons, he'd have long since given up and left the museum. He'd head out to the closest bar and try his luck with another person who catches his eye.

Bailey takes the elevator back upstairs, heads into the back room again—*Ulysses and sirens* waiting for her. But no one else. Her hand is in her bag, hovering over her burner phone—hovering over the send button, which will go directly to Seth, in case the young guy reappears. In case anyone does.

For now, she is safe. She can't be certain, but she is certain enough.

She takes a seat on the bench in front of the *Ulysses* painting, where her father is supposed to meet her.

She feels the panic starting to rise. What if she missed him? What if something happens and he can't come to her? What if the plan is altered, again, before he gets to her? But she closes her eyes against it.

Three breaths. She takes three breaths in and out, just like Hannah taught her. Hannah's voice running through her mind, her heart.

Then she does the hardest thing she knows how to do.

She sits there and she waits.

The Middle Road to Èze Goes One Way

Here's what I know.

When Bailey was sixteen, we lost her father and I started taking notes in a sketchbook. Kind of a teenage version of a baby book. A record of her life.

At first, I was just keeping tabs on her big moments: her high school graduation, that first winter break home from college when we said goodbye to the floating home, the first vacation we took with Charlie and Nicholas. Her dorm room move-ins and move-outs. That first night in her Abbot Kinney apartment.

I told myself that the sketchbook was for Bailey—to give to her one day. But somewhere in my mind I think I knew that it was for Owen, it was always for Owen too, if he ever found his way home again.

The sketchbook that was meant to live between the two bookends—the day Owen left, the day he came back.

As if it gets to be that simple. Nothing is simple when, at sixteen, Bailey lost her father. And, at twenty-two, it's possible she may have him again. Possible, not certain. Far from certain. If I've learned anything over these last five years, it's that nothing gets to feel certain. And it feels like it could jinx her—could jinx all of us—to believe the opposite.

"She's strong," Nicholas says. "That's because of you."

"I don't know about that," I say.

We are back on the motorway, heading toward Èze. Nicholas is driving, his eyes on the road. I turn and look at him, take in his profile, trying to pull myself out of it: where Bailey is, what is about to transpire for her.

"I think that you're giving me too much credit," I say. "She came out that way."

"People come out all sorts of ways," Nicholas says. "Staying that way . . . that's where the testament is."

"Well, that's a testament to her father then," I say. "He was there with her long before I was."

Nicholas nods, taking that in, a color passing over his face. It's a strange mix of melancholy and sadness and something else I don't understand entirely hiding in his eyes—something like guilt.

"How did he seem?" I ask.

"Owen?"

I nod. "I haven't even asked you . . ." I say. "When you were with him, when you were together, how did he seem?"

"What's the answer you're looking for?" he asks.

"What's the truth?"

He pauses, as if considering it—what the answer is. Maybe because the truth is complicated. I could sense that, even from the brief moment Owen was in front of me again at the Design Center, not quite like himself anymore. Though what did that even mean? Wasn't he not like himself when I knew him?

"He seems like he needs you," Nicholas says.

I flinch against that, the gravity of Nicholas's words. And I turn away from him, turning away from a conversation that we can't really have yet, not with what appears just beyond the dashboard.

A sign for Èze on the roadside in front of us, 2 KILOMETERS, like a reminder that we are getting close. As if I need that reminder.

The First Time I Saw Him

"You see down there?"

Nicholas motions over the cliffside, in the direction of the beach far below. I follow his eyes toward the gorgeous cliffside, green and lush and cavernous. Homes dot the hillside—their old French architecture and Mediterranean roofs, windows looking out bright and wide over the Mediterranean Sea.

"I do..."

"Frank's is one of the only houses closer to the water," he says. "Can you see down that far?"

I roll down the window and lean out a bit, scanning the cliffside and the rocks far below. And I can make it out down by the water's edge. There are train tracks, and what looks like a small station beside them, a few lone houses farther down the road, stunning and isolated. And that beachfront—the bright blue water against the sand—completely untouched. It's so beautiful that I could forget what we are doing here. Almost.

"I can see what drew him here," I say. "The serenity, the peace. A perfect antidote, I'd imagine, to how he was living."

"Certainly a lot worse places to try to be a better person," he says.

"Is that what he's been doing here?"

"Maybe in part," Nicholas says.

But his voice tightens as he says this, and I see it flash in his eyes before he can hide it. The anger there. The anger that, after all this time, Nicholas is forced to be here, relitigating the safety of the people that matter the most to him.

"You think that Frank has that kind of conscience?" I ask.

Nicholas doesn't hesitate. "No," he says. "I'm just hoping that I do."

Eight Years Ago

Frank pulled the car over at the small train station, by the side of the road, a rocky beach visible in the distance. It was an unassuming little train station—a two-story red building. The only sign was a plaque near the front door. ÈZE-SUR-MER STATION.

"Let's walk," Frank said to Nicholas. "I want to show you something."

They headed toward that rocky beach, Nicholas reluctantly following him. Frank had been in France on a family vacation for the better part of August. He was staying at that beautiful villa in Cap Ferrat—the one he'd taken Nicholas's family to all those years ago, back when Jenny was still with them. Back when Meredith was still with them. Their wives. All their collective kids. A lifetime ago.

For this extended vacation, only Frank's oldest daughter had joined him. Quinn and her boys. Frank had invited Nicholas to join them as well—Nicholas and Charlie and the twins.

At first, Nicholas had declined. For one thing, it was the first anniversary of Meredith's death, and Nicholas was planning to spend it in Tuscany on the small farm where his wife's grandmother had grown up. And where his wife was now buried.

Meredith and Nicholas had always talked about spending time there when Kate and Charlie were grown. That was always the plan. It wasn't the plan for Meredith to be buried there before they could.

And it certainly wasn't conceivable—not to Nicholas—that his beloved Kate was also buried there, beside her mother.

But this was what had happened. That was Nicholas's reality. Which was partially why, at the last minute, Nicholas decided to fly over and meet Frank instead of going to the farm. To take Frank up on the invite to the South of France.

He couldn't face that farm in Italy, not yet. He couldn't spend his days alone with the two gravestones of the people who mattered most to him.

Was it simply that it would make him feel too sad? Maybe that was part of it. But that wasn't all of it. How could he explain it? He felt like he didn't deserve it yet—the respite that special farm provided. He felt like he could only spend time there when he could truly rest. But his granddaughter was still missing. His heart was still shattered. Nicholas was nowhere near rest, at least not yet.

"This is it," Frank said.

They were at the start of the rocky beach. They crossed the road, followed the unlined crosswalk, and headed to a hiking trail—a sign beside it, naming it. SENTIER NIETZSCHE. The Nietzsche Path.

"This hike here will take us straight up into the village of Èze," Frank said. "It's about three miles, give or take. But you won't feel it."

"Looks like I'll feel it."

"Not at all. I can tell you that. Most gorgeous path you've ever walked. What do you think? You up for a walk?"

"Right now?"

"What's better than now? There are a group of octogenarians who swear by it. They walk the path every day. The three miles up to the village, then back down. One of them is pushing ninety. It's the path and this town and the air here. They swear that it will keep you young forever."

The First Time I Saw Him

"Nothing will keep us young."

"Well I need to show you a house about a quarter of a mile up. Mediterranean, cliffside. It's got these large windows that the current owners call *fenêtres de verité*. Windows of truth. And they tell me that you've never seen a sunset like the one you get there. I think we should hang around, see if they're right."

"Why's that? You thinking of buying it?"

"I already bought it. And the house next door."

"You're joking."

Frank shook his head. "No," he says. "So how about it?"

"How about what?"

"Any desire to take the second house off my hands? Would be a nice place for us to spend our summers."

"Are you serious, Frank? I thought you were just trying to get me to hike up this mountain trail."

Frank gave him a smile, and Nicholas almost added that if he moved anywhere in Europe, it wouldn't be here. He would move to Meredith's grandmother's farm in Tuscany. But he didn't feel like sharing this with Frank. He wasn't up for sharing that with anyone. That place belonged to his family alone.

"One thing at a time," Frank said. "We're going to walk this trail right now and I'm going to take you to La Chèvre d'Or for the best lunch you've ever had and we'll stop by the houses on the way back..."

"I'm never listening to you again when you tell me to put on a pair of sneakers," Nicholas said.

"Does make it harder to find a good excuse to turn around."

Frank started to head up the steep path, but Nicholas stood still. He stared at the trees and the train station and the beach below. And then he looked up at the town itself. Cliffside and luminous, up in those clouds in the late morning light. And then he looked over at his friend in that light. His friend who turned back and was waiting for him.

"What's that look?" Frank asked.

Nicholas didn't answer at first, trying to figure out what he wanted to ask him. Or, rather, trying to figure out how to ask him about what he saw in Frank's eyes—the sadness there. The guilt.

"You think you'll be able to outrun it here?" Nicholas asked.

"Who says I'm trying to outrun anything?"

"No? So it's just me then?"

Frank laughed. "This is Nietzsche country and I like to think we get to play by his rule book," he said. "You know what he always said. No need to outrun your sins. They're not even sins."

"Is that what he said?"

"I'm paraphrasing but, sure. More or less . . ." Frank looked up toward the cliffside, as if trying to recall it, Nietzsche's actual words. "How did he say it? *Whatever is done for love always occurs beyond good and evil.*"

"That sounds like an excuse."

"Maybe . . ." Frank said. But he turned back around. He turned toward Nicholas. "But it's our best shot."

The Sirens Have a Story to Tell Part 2

Ten minutes from closing and the museum is still busy.

Bailey hasn't left the bench. She ignores the tourists who stream in and out of the back room, tries not to make eye contact with any of them.

She keeps her eyes on the painting, studying it. The blues and the green light, the abstract faces of the sirens themselves. It's breathtaking. And she knows it's not a coincidence that her father picked this painting, the bench in front of it, as the place for her to wait.

For her eighth-grade English class, Bailey did a project on the *Odyssey*. She waited until the night before to start. She'd been distracted with the eighth-grade musical (she was playing Hope in *Anything Goes*). She'd been distracted by dress rehearsals and a last-minute recasting of Billy. She was rehearsing her song day and night. She was never without her tap shoes.

Plus she really didn't like her eighth-grade English teacher, Ms. Lofton. She tended to put off the work that Ms. Lofton expected them to do.

Owen was not impressed with this excuse (with any of these excuses) when she woke him up at eleven that night to take her to the store to get poster board. And markers. And glue. And, also, everything else. They had to drive all the way into Marin proper to even find an all-night FedEx store open where they could buy supplies.

Bailey ended up staying up all night to get the project done, Owen staying up with her. He made them plenty of snacks and brewed fresh coffee, playing records to keep them moving. He didn't give her any grief for that though—not that night, not after. He joked that he was too tired to give her any grief.

But Bailey knew that wasn't it. Owen had shown her enough times that he was the person who was never going to give her grief—not when what she was asking for was that he figure out how to do it. To show up for her.

This is when he does.

Again, like always, Owen sits down next to her. He sits down on the bench, leaving a little space between them.

Bailey keeps her eyes on the painting—Owen's eyes focused on the painting too. It doesn't matter. She can feel that it's him before she lets herself look over at him. She doesn't need to look at him to know it's true. It's his skin and his face and his body.

Her heart starts beating hard against her chest, catching in her throat. Making it hard to breathe. To hold herself steady. Her heart starts moving so quickly she thinks she may pass out, right there.

She has the thought: *If I do, he will catch me.* For the first time in a long time, he will be here to catch her.

Owen clears his throat, but he doesn't say anything. Not at first.

She knows that he is waiting to see how she wants this moment to go. He is giving her this moment. He is waiting to see if she wants to hit him or scream or walk away. As if she could walk away, now. He is waiting in a way that tells her it is all okay with him. She knows that any of it is okay with him, because he gets to be by her side again.

She can't look over. She can't make herself do that yet.

"Can't believe that after all that work, Ms. Lofton gave me a B on that project . . ." she says. "I was robbed."

The First Time I Saw Him

"Were you? My memory is you were lucky to get that."

She lets out a small laugh, almost in spite of herself. And she can feel it, the smile starting to break out on his face.

Out of the corner of her eye, she catches it though. She catches what Owen is fighting against at the same time—beneath that small laugh.

She turns toward her father. The first time she is looking at him. His hair is different and his face more angular, rigid, the skin pulled around his mouth. He looks older and too thin and worn down. He looks sad, a sadness she isn't used to seeing in his face. But his eyes, the emotion there, is the same. It's him. Undeniably him.

Her eyes fill with tears, taking him in. Finally taking him in. And suddenly she is five years old again. She is five and she is six and eight. She is running down the docks toward him. She is ten years old and they are flying to New York City for her birthday weekend to see her first Broadway show. She is twelve and he is taking her into downtown San Francisco (hiking her down there every weekend) for voice lessons with a teacher she begged to take lessons from. She is fifteen and being awful to Hannah and being forgiven. Because he would forgive her for anything. He wouldn't even call it forgiveness. He would just call it love.

Which makes it harder. What happens at sixteen. Sixteen and he is teaching her to drive. Sixteen, and like that, he is gone.

Bailey holds that too. She will have to make peace with it, one way or another, but that is for another day. Today she is twenty-two and he is back. And if tonight goes to plan, he will be here, with her, for twenty-three.

Bailey clears her throat, moves closer to him.

"I hear we have a boat to catch," she says.

He nods. "We do."

He still isn't looking back at her, not directly. His eyes holding on the bench, filling up with tears. The tears he can't stop, not anymore.

This is when her father reaches over.

And Bailey takes his hand.

Witching Hour in the Viper's Nest

Mets Vins Chics is a family-owned restaurant just down the hill from Èze's main village.

It's a popular restaurant with locals and tourists alike. There's a full bar and a large outdoor patio surrounded by coral trees and a local piano man regularly playing straight through happy hour.

But, most importantly, it's right next door to Èze's municipal police station.

We park in a space directly in front of that police station.

Then we start to move.

We go into the restaurant and order two glasses of wine, which sit untouched between us. It gives us a chance to use the restroom and freshen up. Nicholas carries his garment bag inside, and I have a dress in my duffel bag (long, black, simple).

I slip the dress on, brushing my hair out, taking stock of myself in the bathroom mirror. I'm wearing the last few days on my face and do my best to mask it, splashing water on my skin, applying some lipstick and mascara. I'm doing what I can so I recognize the person staring back at me. My eyes popping back to life, my hair falling over my shoulders. I take a deep breath and force a smile at my reflection, which is its own form of armor.

When I step out of the bathroom, I find Nicholas waiting by the table. He is in a sports jacket, no tie, a nice pair of pants. He looks broad and sure of himself—and stronger than I've seen him in a while. He looks ready.

"You clean up nice," I say.

"I was about to say the same thing to you."

Nicholas holds the door open and we head outside. But we don't get back in the car.

We drop our bags in the trunk and we head, on foot, out of the parking lot and up the winding hill toward the main village, the cobblestones catching under my heels. We pass the entrance to the Nietzsche Path—that long trail between the seaside and the village, Frank's home on the cliffs in between. The gardens beside it.

We keep going, heading toward the steps that lead into the main village itself.

The steps are steep and wiry, and I can hear it in Nicholas's breath, as soon as we start climbing them. As much as he tries to hide it from me, I can tell that he's struggling with the incline, the wear and tear on his lungs, on his heart. It's visible on his face—what this walk is taking out of him.

It wouldn't do any good to name it, certainly not now. So I walk slower instead. I walk slower in a way that lets him keep going.

We hit the final steps, and the village lays out before us. How can I explain? It's like taking a step back in time. No cars. Just these winding cobblestone streets that can barely fit two rows of people let alone cars.

"Not bad, huh?" Nicholas asks.

"It's so quiet," I say.

"It's mostly a day city. Tourist town. But after dark, especially this time of year . . . not much is going on . . ."

"Especially when one family takes all the available hotel rooms?"

The First Time I Saw Him

"Exactly. There's not a lot of reason to be here at night to begin with. And especially not when you have nowhere to stay over. There's also Èze's town motto."

"And what's that?"

"'In death, I am reborn.'"

"That's ominous," I say.

"Well, it certainly doesn't lend itself to a lot of nightlife . . ."

I start to laugh, turning toward him in a much needed moment of levity. But then I see it on his face. He's still winded from those stairs. From the drive here—from all of this. He's winded in a way that makes me want to insist that he turn around. Except he'll never listen. I know he'll never listen.

So instead, I just take his arm. I take his arm in a way that suggests I'm inviting him to be chivalrous, the two of us continuing down the path together. But it's really so I can keep him closer to me, in my grasp.

We head down the cobblestone path, a fog setting in, a strong breeze, the quiet increasingly eerie.

And I have that feeling—the feeling I've come to know all too well since Owen disappeared. Since I was left to handle the moments of trepidation on my own.

For me—and, most importantly, for Bailey.

It comes up when I sense it: I'm getting closer to something threatening, something that won't be stopped. That I'm about to run into it, the last moment before it's too late to turn back.

"I guess this is what it means to walk into the viper's nest," I say.

"We've been in it, kid," Nicholas says. "At least now we may have a way out."

The Garden in the Sky

The awning at the main entrance to the hotel leads us down a narrow outdoor passageway.

The rock walls close in around us as we pass hotel rooms, winding us toward the hotel restaurant. One way in, the only way back out.

The sole thing to signify our arrival is a small sign with a golden goat, the restaurant name beneath it, Le Café du Jardin—a garden suspended in the sky.

Two people stand beside that sign, by that goat: a hostess with a clipboard in her hands, and a lone security guard in a black suit. An earpiece in his ear.

I don't know what I expect when we get there, but I certainly thought there would be more security than this. More than two people who are more welcoming than frightening, a smile breaking out on the hostess's face.

"*Bonjour*," the hostess says. "*Nous sommes fermés pour une soirée privée . . .*"

Soirée privée. A private party.

"Oui . . ." Nicholas says. *That's what we are here for.* "Nicholas Bell."

"Ah . . ." She looks down at her list, searching until she lands on his name. She checks it off.

"Welcome," she says. "Monsieur Bell."

The security guard steps forward. He puts his hand out and points to my messenger bag.

"I'll need to check your bag first, miss," he says, his American accent thick, the Texas lilt rising up from behind it.

"Of course," I say.

I sound casual, but I feel my stomach roll as I hand him the bag, knowing what's inside. What he will certainly find inside. This security guard that Frank has brought all the way from home with him.

The guard reaches in and moves my things around. Then he pulls out exactly what I don't want him to pull out. What I'm carrying for us—what Nicholas and I need to give to Frank. The tablet.

The tablet is turned off, but the guard turns it over in his hands and I worry that he is going to turn it on—demand the passcode to inspect what's on there. If he does, if he sees what is on there, this will all end here.

"Sorry," I say. "I'm a bit of an overprotective mom, if I'm being honest, and that feeds to my kid's room. Please don't judge me for it. I get enough grief from my husband about letting our son live his life."

I force a laugh. Then I point to Nicholas, trying to sell it.

"It's his grandkid and he's always making fun of me too. I wish I could tell you that he's still a baby and that was my excuse, but he's eight now . . ."

He is still looking at the tablet, as if trying to decide whether to turn it on—whether to just take it away. I can hear the words he is toying with—the decision he is toying with. *You can pick this up after the party. No devices allowed.*

I jump in to stop it. To stop him.

"Do you have kids?" I say.

He doesn't look up. But he answers. He does answer.

The First Time I Saw Him

"Three," he says. "Older than yours."

"Tell me when it gets easier."

"Not so far . . ." he says.

And then, like a miracle, he hands me back the tablet. "This has got to stay off, understood?" he says. "Can't be used for recording anything on the veranda."

"Of course," I say.

But it's like the guard doesn't hear me, or at least he doesn't care. He turns toward Nicholas—as if he will be the one to enforce it, to enforce me.

"We'll keep it off," Nicholas says.

"Phones need to stay in airplane mode too. There is to be no recording on the patio, or anywhere during the party. No photographs."

Nicholas nods. And then the guard steps out of the way, Nicholas motioning for me to go first as we walk through the sliding doors, entering the bar area.

"That wasn't great," I say. I keep my voice low.

"It was expected."

"It didn't feel expected," I say.

"Well, you handled it, so thank you for that."

"What would you do if they had taken you off the list?"

"I was hoping not to find out. But, based on that little display, I'm sure you would have thought of something . . ."

I start to give him a smile, offer a little laugh, but he is focused as we walk into the restaurant's bar.

It's a small and regal room with thick carpet, brick walls, and stained glass windows—medieval flags wrapped around the ceiling. Tonight it's being used as a greeting area. A waiter welcomes us with a tray of champagne flutes and tall glasses of sparkling water.

Nicholas takes two flutes of the champagne, handing me one.

I take a sip and pull my nerves together as we head outside to the staircase leading down to the veranda.

Even in this precipitous moment, it's impossible not to notice the breathtaking views.

This stunner of a garden restaurant perched high above the cliffs of Èze, the Mediterranean Sea spread out far below, the peninsula jutting out, sailboats twinkling in the distance.

And the veranda itself, where the family party is in full swing: kids running around, adults racing after them, music playing and drinks being poured, cocktail tables lit up with tea candles and rustic lanterns.

The feeling in this party surprises me: the lightness, the joy. And what's striking is that it could be any family. Rather, any family who could afford to be standing on top of the Mediterranean Sea celebrating an eightieth birthday.

For a moment, we could be any two other guests, any close friends of the family—standing at the top of the small flight of stairs, entering the party. But then, people start to look up and notice us.

Or, I should say, they notice Nicholas. They are focused on Nicholas, a murmur making its way through some of the family.

But Nicholas doesn't seem to notice them. He isn't interested in any of the chaos around us—the kids racing around, the adults starting to stare at him—as he heads down the flight of steps and onto the veranda.

And whatever uneasiness he was showing outside—whatever vulnerability I was concerned about—it's disappeared.

Nicholas's eyes are steely cold—steely cold and focused and ready. And I recognize it in that readiness: This is what happens when you've saved all your energy to do the thing that matters the most.

The First Time I Saw Him

He is entirely focused on the other end of the veranda, on one person. The only person who matters.

Frank stands in the far corner, in a perfectly tailored linen jacket and jeans—his shoulders wide and broad. He doesn't look eighty. He looks a decade younger than that—everything about him still confident and strong and together.

Frank is in an intimate conversation with a younger man, whose back is to us. A man who is taller than Frank: tall and lanky. Frank's hand reaching up to touch his shoulder—Frank staring at him lovingly.

When the younger man turns, I see that it's Teddy. Teddy, who is also in a sports jacket and jeans, looking like a mirror image of his father (handsome, chiseled, secure). His father to whom he is leaning in close.

This is when I see who is standing behind them. Four security guards in black suits—matching the guard who just searched my bag by the front entrance. Who almost stopped all of this.

They are standing discreetly behind Frank, but near to him all the same. Near enough to intervene.

Near enough to protect him.

If this worries Nicholas, he isn't showing it. He isn't focused on the security guards or Frank's kids. He is, still, entirely focused on Frank.

And maybe Frank feels Nicholas's focus, because he looks up. He looks up and locks eyes with Nicholas.

And he looks at him like he's seeing a ghost.

Which is when it occurs to me, in his mind, he is.

Nicholas squeezes my arm as we make our way toward them. Teddy follows his father's glare in Nicholas's direction. He does a double take. Then he turns toward me, his eyes scanning my legs and dress and my hair. I know there are a lot of women who may find him good-looking. But the way he is unabashedly eyeing me makes me certain that no one knows that better than he does.

What's almost worse than his unapologetic lasciviousness is what's lingering behind that gaze, behind his eyes, which are bloodshot and vacuous. Something like an emptiness—a blankness. It makes me eager to turn away from him, but I don't let myself. I will not be the one to blink first.

Frank, meanwhile, is still locked onto Nicholas.

"Well, this is a surprise," Frank says.

"Happy Birthday, Frank . . ."

"I didn't think you were going to make it," Frank says. "On account of the fact that you're supposed to be dead."

"Yeah. Sorry for the confusion there."

Frank laughs, soft and genuine. But he is still staring at Nicholas, confused. And I think they're going to shake hands, but Frank leans in and holds Nicholas to him, the hug of longtime friends. Of brothers.

Frank pulls back, and the two men hold eyes—neither of them wanting to break. Until Frank turns, nods in my direction.

"And this must be Hannah . . ."

I nod. Even though Frank isn't asking. He knows who I am. But if he wonders what I'm doing here, he doesn't let on. He is too focused on what Nicholas is doing here—Nicholas, who he believed was lost to him.

Everyone else seems to be wondering too—about Nicholas and maybe about me. They're also less invested in hiding their confusion than Frank is. Teddy is still eyeing me. The conversations nearby lowering to a softer din, the security guards moving in closer.

In my periphery, I see a woman heading toward us from where she was holding court a few feet away.

Quinn. She is dressed in a red pantsuit, chunky Christian Louboutin

The First Time I Saw Him

heels, her blond hair pulled back in a low bun. She is elegant and striking at once. Those heels adding even more inches to her six-foot-tall frame.

She has disengaged from the conversation she was in, to move closer to us. To be standing by Frank's side. Quinn now on one side of him, Teddy on the other. The two of them flanking their father. The guards right behind them.

"What the hell is going on here?" she says.

"Nice to see you too, Quinn," Nicholas says.

But Nicholas doesn't look at Quinn when he says it. He doesn't look at Teddy or at Quinn. He keeps his eyes firmly on Frank.

"Nicholas," Quinn says. "Care to explain yourself?"

"You should really feel free to go first," Nicholas says. "You and Teddy here . . ."

"What the fuck is that supposed to mean?" Teddy asks.

Frank puts his hand on his son's arm, silencing him. "Let's find a better place to have this discussion, yeah?"

"That's your call, Frank," Nicholas says. "But you should probably know, we're on a clock."

"A clock?" Frank asks.

"The local police know we're here," Nicholas says. "And while it's safe to assume you're not particularly worried about the municipal police in Èze . . ."

"I wouldn't say so, no."

"That's fair," Nicholas says. "But I imagine that this little party cost you somewhere north of seven figures. And you don't want half a dozen officers barging in here and turning it into a scene."

Frank lets out a small laugh, as if this is all an irritation. But I see something behind it that he is trying to hide. His anger. And something else. Something I can't properly put my finger on yet.

"Plus, it's less the police and more what one particular officer there has been paid quite well to do."

"And what's that, Nick?" Teddy asks.

"He'll be making a call to my associate, who has been instructed that if Hannah and I don't walk out of here safely at exactly the twenty-minute mark, a series of documents will be sent simultaneously to Agent Grady Bradford in the Eastern District of Texas US Marshals Service and to the head of the criminal division of the US attorney's office Southern District of Florida."

"You're full of shit . . ." Teddy says.

"Afraid not, Teddy. And if these documents are sent, you will be arrested as soon as you step foot back in the United States . . ." Nicholas continues, his voice steady. "I've been assured of that."

"Have you lost your fucking mind?" Quinn asks. Her face is getting red with anger, her voice anything but steady.

"You too, Quinn . . ." Nicholas says. "All three of you, actually. Not to mention most of your siblings."

"You have," she says. "You've lost your fucking mind."

"*Enough*," Frank says.

His voice is sharp, angry. Which is enough, apparently, for Quinn and Teddy to step off. To quite literally step back.

Though something seems to shift.

Frank moving closer to Nicholas. He smiles at him, but it's a terrible smile. "What are you starting here, old friend?"

"I didn't start this. Your children did when they decided not to honor the understanding you and I came to," he says. "For reasons I'm uninterested in, they started this when they put a bounty on my granddaughter."

Frank's smile disappears. And he turns toward his children, his

The First Time I Saw Him

eyes cold. And menacing. And I know that Nicholas was correct—that whatever Quinn and Teddy authorized here, Frank was not a part of it. He wasn't a part of that decision to move against our family, not in the way that he would have wanted to be.

Teddy leans in toward Frank. "Could we have a moment alone with you?" he says. "Please?"

"Probably needs to wait, son," Nicholas says. "We've got just a little over eighteen minutes until you're going to jail."

This is when Teddy lunges, actually lunges, at Nicholas—and I raise my arm to block him.

It's instinctual—how fast I move. My arm is in front of Nicholas's face—my whole body in front of him—the force of Teddy's blow landing squarely on my jaw.

This sets off Frank's guards, who move closer to us, surrounding us, until it is there. A gun against my ribs. Its barrel cold and unmitigated. The first time in my life I've felt that, as sudden and impossible a thing as I've ever felt.

My heart moves into my throat, quick and fierce. My jaw pounding, my ribs pounding. Right up against the gun.

I look around the veranda, waiting for someone to intervene. But everyone is suddenly looking somewhere else. No one is looking at Nicholas, or at me. No one wants to bear witness to any of it: the gun against my rib; the guard's breath and sweat, tight against my skin; his two companions holding on tight to Nicholas. Eighty people around us and we may as well be alone. No one will do a thing to step in. Not for either of us.

I can taste the blood in my mouth, on the inside of my cheek. The sting growing more intense. My jaw pulsing. This is what real danger feels like, isn't it? It doesn't announce itself at the door. It creeps up behind you until there's nothing you can do but try—with everything you've got left—to breathe into it.

I focus in on Nicholas, who looks calm. He looks calmer than I've ever seen him. It levels me out. The guy who was out of breath on the steps is no longer here. The only version of Nicholas present here is strong and unfazed: the guy who orchestrated this confrontation, ready to show everyone why.

"Move them away from Hannah, Frank," Nicholas says. "Everyone needs to step back. Right fucking now."

Frank keeps his eyes on Nicholas. Calculating. Then he nods toward his security, and the guards immediately pull back.

They let go of Nicholas—and the guard on me takes the gun off my ribs, the skin where the barrel just was, raw and pounding. My eyes hold on the guards back in their corner, their hidden guns. On the small distance between us.

Frank turns and takes me in, his eyes giving nothing away at first. But I think I see a flash of it in his face—concern for me—my jaw, red and throbbing. But maybe that's what I want to see.

"We're not doing this here . . ." Frank says.

Then he motions toward a private room on the edge of the veranda. Nicholas nods, and we head that way.

I hold my hand to my jaw, try to cup it, cool it out—the pounding pain, my heart beating through it.

But Frank puts up his hand, blocks me from following.

"No, just Nicholas. I'd like to discuss this with him alone . . ." he says. Then he motions toward Quinn and Teddy. "You two stay here. Keep Ms. Hall company."

"Not possible, Frank," Nicholas says. "They're coming too."

"And why is that?"

"This involves them now. They made sure of that."

The First Time I Saw Him

Quinn glares at Nicholas. She is glaring at both of us, like her father's displeasure with her is our fault. Like she'd will the guns back on our ribs, if she could, as punishment for that alone.

"I would say so . . ." she says.

Frank meets Nicholas's eyes, but it feels private. Not like a warning, more like a plea. Like he is unhappy that Nicholas is involving Quinn—that he is choosing to do this in a way that's not just the two of them.

"You better know what you're doing here, Nicky," Frank says.

"Haven't I always?"

"Maybe not always."

"Sixteen minutes."

"Follow me."

This Slip Is Spoken For

Owen could be anywhere.

His back is to the water.

He is surrounded by computer screens and monitors. He has tracking devices on eighteen people and two police stations and encrypted calls set to deploy to the municipal police and the US consulate in Nice and a certain US marshal in the eastern district of Texas in conjunction with the Southern District of Florida.

He has everything covered, as much as it's possible to have it covered. He is confident of that. He's run it out, too many times to even count, every possible scenario for how the next sixteen minutes will go. How the night needs to go after that. Every possible scenario to get them all to safe harbor.

Especially Hannah.

Especially Bailey.

Bailey, who is in the cabin next to him. He can hear the shower going, can hear her music kicking out of the speakers. He wanted to give her a minute to herself—to process, to take a breath, to settle back into herself.

He's even put a keyboard in her cabin so she can begin to work on her music if she wants to do that. Anything she wants to do to help keep herself together, until he brings Hannah home to her.

It's taking everything that he's got not to knock on that cabin door, to wait for her to let him in so he can take another look at her.

To make her a cup of peppermint tea or ask her to play him a song on that keyboard. Or do anything at all so that he gets to watch her for a bit. To prove to himself that she's here. She's safe.

It's taking him back to it, a little too viscerally. It takes him back to their first night in the floating home. Their first night in their new life. It was a few months before Bailey's fifth birthday—five weeks and five days after they had first run from Austin, and the organization, and the life he couldn't protect Bailey from. He had failed, after all, to protect Kate. The price of that, the pain of it, living on his daughter's face. He wasn't going to make that mistake again, not with their kid.

At the same time, he'd had no interest in a life in which he was at the mercy of WITSEC and government bureaucracy to protect him—a life in which Owen would constantly be looking over his shoulder. You could argue that the same was true with the path Owen has chosen. But at least, doing it this way, Owen wasn't counting on anyone but himself.

That first night in the floating home, Bailey had wanted to sleep in her own room, which he'd filled with her favorite things: Hello Kitty pillows and oversize LEGOs and Cinderella coloring books. It was the only room Owen had managed to decorate, at all.

Owen was relieved that Bailey felt safe enough to be in there on her own—that she'd wanted that. It made him feel like he had managed to hide it from her—just how much danger they were actually in.

And still. Owen sat outside her bedroom door all night. He didn't even have a blanket over him, the chill of the mostly empty houseboat helping him to stay awake.

He was trying to imagine a day when keeping watch like that wouldn't be what was required of him—in order to keep his family safe.

The First Time I Saw Him

Apparently, nearly two decades later, he doesn't have that answer. Not just yet. Not tonight.

Owen closes his cabin door. He takes a seat at the desk. His computer screens power on. His monitors kick up, their blue light shining back at him. The encrypted phone lines ready. It all comes to life.

Five years, ten months, and twenty-seven days.

It's time.

No One's Hands Are Clean

"Teddy, pour everyone a drink," Frank says.

We are sitting in the back room, a small dining room off the veranda. It's apparently only used when the weather is poor, when they can't have dinner reservations outside. It hasn't been used in a long time. No tablecloths. No pretty lights shining over the large windows. Chairs folded up.

The opposite of the party twelve feet away.

Frank's security guards pulled the chairs down around a corner table—a rectangular six-top. Nicholas and I sit on one side of the table, Quinn and her father on the other. Teddy walking over from the small bar.

The guards, meanwhile, stand on the other side of the room—by the door leading out to the veranda, to the party. They're making sure no one else is coming in—or that any of us, apparently, are getting out.

Somehow it doesn't make this all seem safer.

Teddy hands his father a bourbon, taking the free seat next to him. Frank doesn't say thank you. He doesn't even look at Teddy. He looks only at Nicholas as he takes a long sip of the drink, leans back calmly in his chair.

"Nicholas," he says, "I would think you would be the last person I'd need to tell that issuing threats is not the way to negotiate with us."

"We aren't negotiating," Nicholas says. "We already negotiated and your children broke that agreement."

"So what is this then?"

"A delivery," he says.

I pull the tablet out of my bag, rest it on the table. But I don't pass it over. Not to Frank—nor Teddy, nor Quinn. Not yet.

"As I mentioned," Nicholas continues, "we have a large number of documents that we feel confident you would rather remain . . . in your family. That I have devoted my life to keeping away from anyone who is not in your family."

He looks at Frank when he says this part. He looks at Frank and holds his eyes.

Frank doesn't ask what kind of documents. He doesn't need to ask. They are the kind of documents and data that Nicholas has collected over decades of working with Frank. Documents that detail every indiscretion, every illegal activity, every capital crime. The documents that Nicholas went to jail for (for the better part of ten years) as opposed to producing them for the authorities.

"All the files have been collated and organized by year and criminal wrongdoing, cross-labeled to highlight individual culpability, redacting any criminal activity for which statute of limitations has expired. As you know, that doesn't apply to most of them . . ." he says. "A flash drive has been delivered to each of your homes. Just so everyone is on the same page as to what we are talking about."

"But you were our lawyer," Quinn says.

"That is true."

"So I can't imagine that I need to remind you that whatever you think you've collected here would all fall under the umbrella of attorney-client privilege. Completely inadmissible in the court of law."

"Well, Quinn, maybe I need to remind you that I haven't been your lawyer for quite a long time," Nicholas says. "Moreover, I was disbarred when I went to prison to protect your family . . ."

"That doesn't necessarily pierce privilege."

"That's arguable. But it's also not relevant. The court found that the nature of my criminal activity, the scope of what I did to protect your family, meant I was not acting in the capacity of your lawyer, but rather as a part of the organization. And that certainly does pierce attorney-client privilege." He pauses as Quinn takes that in. "In fact, it blows any privilege out of the water. Which, as you should know, makes every document on this tablet admissible by the Feds. In whatever capacity they want to use them."

Nicholas nods in my direction and I slide the tablet across the table to Frank.

"Password is 080811 . . ." I say.

Frank looks over at me, and I see him clock it. The significance of the password. Of that date. Of the month and the day.

The day that Kate was killed.

He taps in the password. And the tablet clicks on. The screen divides into six squares, revealing six houses. One house in Indian Creek, one on Fisher Island, two in Silver Lake, one in Nashville, and a final home in downtown Miami. Six live camera streams, into each of those houses. The living rooms and home offices, the kitchens and sunrooms. The basements.

"What the hell is this?" Teddy says.

Because he recognizes those houses. The home in East Nashville (his brother Dominic's home), the two houses down the street from each other on the Reservoir in Silver Lake (the houses belonging to his twin sisters), an apartment in South Miami (his baby brother Bradley's home), the house on Fisher Island (the house belonging to Quinn).

And of course he recognizes, especially, the home streaming in the first box—the Indian Creek home, his home.

"You've been surveilling our fucking houses?" Quinn says.

"Did you not, seventy-two hours ago, have a man at my house?" I say. "And at my kid's place?"

Quinn leans forward toward me—that red suit, her polished hair, all of it still somehow in place.

"All due respect, this all started a long time before you got here," she says.

"Which is why it would have made sense to leave me out of it . . ."

I shoot her a look, refusing to stand down.

"Everything would have gone on exactly as it had been going on," I say. "If you didn't feel the need to break things. To break the seal. Because now you've threatened me. And far worse you threatened my kid. And Nicholas's grandchild. So now it's very much about us. It's about all of us."

"All of us?" Frank says.

"I knew that you weren't particularly trusting of the outside world, Frank, but even I was surprised how much you moved through your children's properties," Nicholas says. "And we have it all. Every wire transfer. Every package coming in and out of each residence. Everything on the home computers. Which means even your younger children, who have decided to start fresh, who, if you will, have tried to stay away from the family business . . . they are implicated too."

Frank's eyes go steely.

"Racketeering. Money laundering, mail fraud. Extortion. Conspiracy. Possession with the intent to distribute. No one's hands are clean."

"I don't need the list."

The First Time I Saw Him

"Nevertheless. It's all in the documents."

Nicholas turns toward Teddy and Quinn. "It's particularly unfortunate that you chose to take that phone call at your brother's condominium in September of last year," Nicholas says. "Even without Bradley's direct knowledge, conspiracy to commit happening on an ADA's property? The Feds won't believe he wasn't involved if you were careless enough to use his home and phone to conduct business. Not just on that occasion. But on five others that we documented."

"Fuck you," Teddy says.

"Fuck me?"

"You are involving innocent people in this."

"I think, Teddy, if anyone should understand involving innocent people, it would be you and your sister . . ." Nicholas says.

Nicholas turns away, but Teddy is still staring at him, confused suddenly. And I see him start to wonder if Nicholas is referring to just the organization coming for Bailey and me. Or, rather, if Nicholas is referring to something else entirely.

Frank stops Teddy. He's heard enough. "This kind of surveillance," he says. "This has been years of planning."

"I guess when you leave someone with nothing," I say. "All they've got is time."

Quinn looks at me. Then she turns away as she starts to put the pieces together. The pieces that lead this all back to Owen. Everything Owen had to do—had to risk—to hack into each of their systems. Everything he was able to get away with. Because at the end of the day he is smarter. He is smarter than all of them.

"So Owen is behind this?" she says.

"One could argue that you are, Quinn," Nicholas says.

"How do you figure that?"

"None of this was put into action until we learned what you intended to do in regard to my family."

She looks down at the tablet, zooms in on her beautiful sunroom, staring back at her. And I can see it going through her mind—everything that may have been witnessed there. And by whom.

"You can thank your son-in-law for anything that is happening to your family," Quinn says.

"I think we're playing way past that at this point," Nicholas says.

"Is that right?"

"Focusing on him isn't particularly serving you. Focusing on the past isn't serving any of us. Not when we all need to focus on what happens now."

"Which is what exactly?" Frank says.

His tone is so quiet and serious that it's almost hard to hear him. As if he wants it to be hard to hear him. As if Frank wants to convey to Nicholas—and only him—what has been started here. What Nicholas has started here. And what the price will be if he doesn't figure out a way to stop it.

"They get to go on with their lives now," Nicholas says. "All of them. Your children. And mine. Charlie and the kids. Hannah and Bailey. And Owen too."

"Owen too?"

"Yes. All of them. This all fucking ends here."

Frank doesn't say anything, not at first.

"If my children were sloppy enough to allow this to happen, who is to say that I care enough about them that I won't just let them go down?"

"Isn't that the one thing we have in common? Even now, Frank?" He pauses. "We'd do anything for our children."

The First Time I Saw Him

Frank meets Nicholas's eyes. He looks him right in the eyes, and he pulls out a gun. He pulls out a gun, and I think he is bluffing. Of course he is bluffing. Isn't this what you do when you are bluffing?

Except then he shoots.

Four Years Ago

They were eating in South Pointe Park, at Frank's favorite steak house. It was just the two of them having dinner, but Frank rented out the back room anyway. The back room with the best views of that special piece of Miami oceanfront.

They were having a birthday dinner—seventy-six for Frank, seventy-one for Nicholas. These were numbers they didn't want to acknowledge, but also were happy to acknowledge. It was several months belated for Nicholas. He had spent his actual birthday with Bailey, the week of her high school graduation. She and Hannah had taken him to their favorite restaurant in the Castro for risotto and Sweetwater oysters and the best lemon cake he'd ever tasted in his life. And soon he would be with them again—the family heading to Hawaii for Christmas, for Bailey's break.

Nicholas would get to be with Bailey for a whole week. He'd have a whole week of getting to watch Bailey being Bailey. It was crazy how much joy that brought him, just watching Bailey be Bailey. It was crazy for him to know that kind of joy again.

Nicholas was filling Frank in on all of it, on Bailey's graduation. On the Hawaii plans. Frank laughing that she was trying to make Nicholas go surfing with him; Frank laughing that Nicholas was going to try and do it.

And Nicholas could see it—how happy Frank was for him. About all of it.

"I'm talking too much. Which I guess is just a way of saying thank you. Thank you for letting me call in that favor."

"Favor?"

Frank looked at him, confused. And Nicholas could see him pulling it up in his memory—that moment all those years ago, two nights before Nicholas reported to prison, when Frank promised him he'd make it up to him. He'd make it up to Nicholas that he was going to prison for Frank. That he was taking that impossible hit.

But now Frank only shook his head.

"That's not the favor . . ."

"No?"

"No. I'd never let your family be hurt. Not on my watch. You deserve safety for your family. You're a good man."

"I don't know that either of us should be talking about what a good man is," Nicholas said.

"That's true too."

Frank smiled at him, but Nicholas felt something twist up inside him. Maybe because Nicholas was leaving something out. They had been at dinner for several hours and Nicholas still hadn't mentioned that Owen had reached out to him.

That went against the agreement they made when Frank said he would protect Hannah and Bailey. Nicholas had promised to let Frank know if Owen contacted him (or if he knew that Owen contacted Hannah or Bailey). He insisted that he'd let Frank know immediately. But here they were and he didn't fill Frank in on the note that Owen left waiting for him in that hotel room in San Francisco.

If something happens to you, they'll be in danger.

Why? Why was he holding this information back from Frank? It certainly wasn't out of any loyalty to Owen. No, that wasn't it.

The First Time I Saw Him

Which gave Nicholas pause: Was it that he wasn't convinced that Owen was wrong?

He flinched against it, the answer that sprung to his mind before he could stop it. He wasn't convinced. And, if that was the case, if even a small piece of Nicholas believed that Owen was correct, that Hannah and Bailey were potentially in danger—what did that mean? What did that mean about what actually happened to Kate? What did that mean about Frank's involvement?

"So, you need to tell me, Frank."

Frank looked at Nicholas, confused.

"Tell you what?"

"Tell me the truth," Nicholas said. "When did you know?"

"Know what?"

"That someone in the organization was behind it," Nicholas said. "Someone was behind what happened to Kate, weren't they?"

"Nick, I would never hurt your kids."

Frank shook his head. And he saw in Frank's eyes that Frank meant that. It was what carried them along all these years—that Frank did, in fact, mean that. So why did Nicholas know suddenly, with a blistering clarity, that this wasn't the whole truth? Was it just Owen reaching out to him?

No. But Nicholas's reaction to Owen's note did spark it. It sparked something that Nicholas knew—the thing we know about lifelong friends if we pay close enough attention to what they are saying. And what they leave out.

Frank had readily agreed to help Hannah and Bailey. How was that not the favor? How did that not make them even? Because they could never be even. That was what Nicholas knew for sure now. That was what a part of him knew all along. A part of him apparently knew before Frank even did.

"What happened, Frank?"

Frank looked down at his coffee, and for a moment Nicholas got to believe that he was wrong. What a relief it would be, to be wrong! But then Frank looked up. And it was like Nicholas could see it coming off Frank's skin—which was reddening and splotchy. He could see what Frank had been keeping in, all this time. What he was finally letting out.

"Let me be clear," he said. "It had nothing to do with your decision to pull back from work. Or with any issues that arose from that. It was nothing punitive." He paused. "It had to do with Kate."

Nicholas felt it, a hitch in his throat. Even at the sound of it now—Frank even saying his daughter's name now.

"Once your son-in-law became involved with your work, with setting up that encryption system, Kate got nervous," Frank continued. "She was nervous Owen could be implicated, even if you kept him in the dark. She was nervous about his culpability."

"How the hell would you know that?"

"She started asking questions at work," Frank said. "She was asking questions in a way that was raising flags."

"Bullshit. She would have come to me."

"Nick, she walked into the US attorney's office and asked an AUSA point-blank if you were under investigation in some way. Which put you on their radar in a new way. And a friend inside the AUSA's office . . . he alerted us."

This stopped Nicholas cold. The new layers of information were shuffling around in his head, trying to find a way to click in. To make sense.

Kate was nervous. She was nervous about what Nicholas had pulled Owen into—nervous enough that she felt she couldn't ask Nicholas himself. That she couldn't trust his response. What did that say about how his daughter was feeling about him, in the end? What did that say about the fear she was holding inside about her husband's safety? The fear that Nicholas was the cause of?

"So you knew?"

"Not me directly. But one of my lieutenants, yes."

"You want me to believe that no one let you know what was going on? Give me a fucking break, Frank."

"It's the truth, Nick."

"No one did anything without you knowing it."

"I didn't authorize it. I swear to God. And the lieutenants who were involved with this, they are no longer walking on this earth . . . needless to say, perhaps, but . . ." He paused. "They were handled as soon as I was made aware."

Nicholas remembered something about that. He was in jail, and he remembered learning that two high-level lieutenants in the organization were taken out. Two lieutenants who Nicholas had represented at trial years earlier. They had been tried for burglary and extortion. Nicholas had gotten them cleared.

This was why he thought that Frank had mentioned their *ending* to him—in the way that Frank relayed these things. The cleaned-up language: they were no longer with the organization. Due to insubordination. How many years after Kate's death did Frank share this? Five years, close to six. Was that how long before Frank knew?

"Someone authorized it, Frank. What happened to my daughter. Someone had to authorize it. These men wouldn't have done this without the explicit blessing of someone in the family."

Frank looked at him, and Nicholas saw it—the way we see things in the people we know best—or, at least, that we've known the longest. Even the things (especially the things) that we wish we could unsee.

"She was just a kid herself, Nick . . ." He shakes his head. "She just authorized them to scare Kate, not to hurt her. Certainly not to kill her."

"Quinn?"

Nicholas asked it as a question. But he had his answer. He started to think that maybe he always had the answer. The way we know things before we are willing to know them. The way we feel the preliminary pain we aren't ready to acknowledge yet.

"We don't control what our children do. I don't need to tell you that. And Quinn . . . she wasn't thinking clearly. She was too wrapped up in her own pain. Her own anger. Her fears that our family was being threatened."

Nicholas nodded. He didn't doubt that. As though that was what mattered now. All that mattered was this: Kate was walking down the street, eager to get home to her daughter, and then, silence. Because of how Nicholas led his life. Because of whom he'd invited into it. That was the point. That was the only point.

"Nick, I promise you on my own children, I did not know then. I didn't know for a long time. I've spent my life sorry about that."

"Not good enough."

"I know."

"I don't care what you know."

Nicholas got up to leave.

"We're done."

In Death, I Am Reborn

Nicholas hits the ground hard.

It vibrates off my skin, the ringing from the shot. I feel it in my ears, everything echoing loudly. I can't hear anything outside of that echo. The world spins fast around me—the pressure destabilizing—pushing me into a tunnel, toward the only thing that matters: Nicholas on the ground, bleeding.

I drop to the floor, so I can study him. So I can ascertain where exactly he was hit and how to quickly help.

He is looking up at me, stunned but conscious. My hands cup his head, which is clean, unbuttoning his suit jacket, palming his chest. Which is when I see the red spreading out near his neck, coming from the top of his shoulder.

I rip open his shirt and reach for a napkin. A cloth napkin. I hold it against the top of his shoulder and apply pressure.

"You're okay," I say.

It's a statement more than a question because it won't stop coming at me—how much I need it to be true.

I pull the napkin away and look at the wound. There doesn't seem to be a bullet lodged there. The skin cut through. Just a slick and awful graze. And still blood colors the napkin, sticks hard to all my fingers.

Nicholas looks up at Frank. "Are you insane?" he asks.

Frank is standing over Nicholas and me, the gun still in his hand. It's down by his side, but still in his hand. Still cocked.

"You two walk in here speaking about mutually assured self-destruction, but I'm the insane one?"

This is when I stand up. And, with everything I've got, I turn to face Frank, holding on to his gaze. Not cowering. Not cowering even with that gun still cocked. Quinn and Teddy standing by their father, the security team ready to follow their boss's cue.

I look at Teddy for just a moment, which is all the time he deserves, Nicholas starting to rise to his feet. He lets out a grunt, quick and guttural—holding tight to that shoulder. But he starts to rise all the same.

He winces—the pain visible on his face—but he fights through it. He fights through the tear in his shoulder, ripping through his skin.

"That's the wrong way to look at this," Nicholas says.

"What's the right way?"

"Everything on that tablet never leaves that tablet. You know that's true. It's never left that tablet, even to my own detriment," he says. "As long as nothing happens to my family, it never will."

Frank moves forward, helping Nicholas the rest of the way up, as though he wasn't the one who just shot him. As though he doesn't still have the gun in his hand, firmly cocked, should he decide to use it again.

"That includes nothing intentional, of course . . ." Nicholas continues. "But nothing unintentional either. Not even an accident. A plane accident. A boat. Anyone in my family gets touched in any way and there is another party that will deploy it."

"We don't control a fucking plane," Teddy says.

"Then I guess you'd better pray," I say.

Teddy shakes his head, agitated. And disbelieving. But he stays silent. He stays silent because what is there to say? He and his sister created this situation. The only question now is how he gets out of it.

The First Time I Saw Him

Frank moves in closer to Nicholas.

"This is why you don't trust someone with everything," Frank says.

"I guess you could say we both learned that."

Frank nods, offers a small smile. It should make me more nervous that Frank is standing so close to Nicholas: the gun still by his side, the security guards with their hands on their pockets. But something in how Frank is watching Nicholas makes me calmer. I slow down—my breathing, my heart—and let myself know it. The graze wasn't an accident. If Frank wanted to kill him, he could have. He wanted to do something else.

"I think it's time, Nick," Frank says. "For that minute alone."

You Can't Plan for
What You Can't Plan For Part 2

This is what Owen learned.

When he started to study everything about Èze to prepare for tonight—the topography and the history and the village—he spent a lot of time learning about Nietzsche. Or, maybe he should say, relearning Nietzsche. Owen had been introduced to his work in the philosophy course he took his junior year at UT-Austin, the smug TA reading aloud full passages from *The Antichrist* that went right over Owen's head.

He's not sure how much more he ingested this time around. But there is no denying that he had to try. They are synonymous with each other in a way—Èze's most famous resident and the medieval village that helped shape him. The village that helped shape *Thus Spoke Zarathustra*, Nietzsche's meditation on mortality. On the physical world and government and power. On forgiveness.

Nietzsche didn't believe in forgiveness. He believed it was a sign of weakness to attempt forgiveness, to ask to be forgiven. How did Nietzsche articulate it? *I forgive you what you have done to me; that you have done it to yourself, however—how could I forgive that!*

Those words have been running through Owen's head, on a strange recurring loop, especially in moments like this. In moments when Owen bumps up against most wanting the opposite to be true.

That, at the end of this, there will be a way for them to forgive him. There will be a way for him to start to forgive himself. Only that involves undoing what he did wrong. It involves making the right choice.

Finally, making the right choice.

But which way is the right choice?

There is one camera feed that is not on the tablet Hannah and Nicholas have—a feed that only Owen has—a feed telling him a different story.

It's a feed coming from the camera on that open tablet, letting him see what is happening in that back room in Èze.

Owen watches Nicholas go down as Hannah bends over him. Owen watches as Nicholas slowly gets back up.

Hannah standing there beside him.

Owen looks at the clock. It's been nineteen minutes. Nineteen minutes and eight seconds. Time is about to be up.

He clicks over to his encrypted calls app, hovers over the numbers waiting to be activated. The number for the US consulate in Nice, and the number to Grady in Austin, and the number to the municipal police.

Owen's contact at the municipal police is standing fifty feet from the awning of the hotel. And the restaurant. And that back room. He has five of his most trusted officers with him. They're ready to race in, ready to save them.

Except that he and Nicholas planned for this. Even for this. Nicholas's words racing to the forefront of his mind. *Stay the course.* What did they agree to? At the moment you think you can't, that's the moment you most need to.

Owen zooms in on Hannah's face—her beautiful face. She doesn't look scared, standing there. She looks certain.

The First Time I Saw Him

And yet it undoes him. Because it all comes down to Hannah, doesn't it? For Owen, it has come down to Hannah since the moment he met her, since that first moment when she turned toward him. And his whole fucking life began again.

Stay the course.

But which way is the course?

Which way does he move now, if he cannot hear her tell him?

The Waiting Room

"Do you have any idea what you've done here?" Quinn says.

We are back on the veranda. I'm standing with Quinn by the outside bar, holding a cold bottle of beer against the side of my face. Holding it against my jaw. My jaw, which is throbbing and angry, the taste of blood still thick and metallic in my mouth.

Quinn stares at me, blank-eyed and completely unsympathetic. I'm not thinking about her though. Not really. I'm thinking about Nicholas.

The bar is as near as we can get to the back room—to whatever is happening in there between Nicholas and Frank. There are no windows looking in on them, no way to see for certain what is going on. The security guards are standing by the door, blocking the only way in. The only way out.

Nicholas is not more than twelve feet away from me—bleeding and injured. It might as well be twelve hundred.

I try to focus on Quinn, on the party happening around us. The party is in full force, like nothing awful is happening.

If anyone even heard the gunshot, you wouldn't know, not from their actions. No one is picking up their kids and racing out. No one is doing anything but enjoying their wine and laughing. Music playing, appetizers being shared: Wagyu beef, porcini mushrooms, seafood platters.

Teddy is somewhere among them, pretending he didn't just watch his father shoot someone. Maybe he's managed to push it out of his mind—to convince himself that it will be handled, one way or another.

So maybe they heard nothing, at all. Maybe they have no idea something awful is happening. Or maybe that's what you have to do to survive in this family—to survive existing on the edge of this kind of peril. You don't see what you're not supposed to see. You get practiced at looking the other way.

"This was all so fucking unnecessary," Quinn says.

She shakes her head as the bartender places a shot of bourbon on the bar top in front of her. She downs it, motions for him to give her another.

I think of the utility workers ready to grab us, of everything that has happened since we chose to run.

"I'd argue the unnecessary part was you sending your henchman to my door. To my kid's apartment," I say. "But sure . . ."

"Please," Quinn says. "Give me a break. Neither of you would have been hurt, just detained."

"Well, I'm sure that would have been very pleasant," I say. "Thank you for that clarification."

"She would have survived it," she says. "You both would have."

"Once you got to my husband, you mean?"

"My point is," she continues, "now this is all something else . . ."

I feel compelled to argue with her, but I know it won't do any good. I know that Quinn has no interest in hearing that this has, in fact, been *something else*—for me, for Bailey, for Owen—for quite a long time. She won't be able to hear me when what she cares about—when all Quinn cares about—is that now it threatens her too.

"Look, Quinn," I say. "I realize that there is a long history here. And that there is no love lost between you and my husband."

The First Time I Saw Him

"You do? You realize that?"

I ignore her tone—her dismissal.

"Regardless . . ." I push on. "My understanding is that for you, at least, this wasn't your original plan . . ."

"What the hell does that mean?"

I cycle through what I know to be true about her—that Quinn only stepped into a leadership position after her husband was sent away. That Owen, in her mind, is the reason that happened. So, perhaps, it isn't just the loss of her husband that she blames Owen for. It's everything else too. It's everything that her life might have been had she been allowed to sit on the sidelines of this world. Everything that her life might have been if fate hadn't stepped in to demand something else of her, to demand that she show up—the way she felt she needed to show up—for her family.

"It means that I understand it," I say. "I understand you not wanting to be involved with your family's business. You were headed in a different direction, correct? College, law school, an associate position at a prestigious law firm . . ."

"You think that means you know me? Because you know some biographical details about my past?"

"No. I would never presume that I know you," I say. "I would just like it if you didn't assume you know me."

She narrows her eyes, and I worry that I've overstepped. That the opening I thought I'd found was the opposite. But then she starts to speak. For the first time, she starts to speak *to* me as opposed to *at* me.

"If what you're getting at is that plans change, then yes," she says. "My plans did change after Wesley was sent away. Which left my brother in charge on his own. My brother, who wasn't equipped to handle the business, on his own . . ."

"I gathered."

She offers a small laugh, almost in spite of herself.

"Then what are you asking me, really?" she says. "Why twenty years later I still blame your husband?"

"No. I can wrap my head around that part," I say. "I assume you blame him because you think he started it."

She doesn't argue. She can't. "Sure . . ."

"But what I'm saying is that you know, as well as I do, that my husband didn't start this," I say. "This started when Kate was killed on the side of the road."

"That was an *accident*," Quinn says.

But she looks upset when she says it. And I can see what she tries to hide on her face when she does—that maybe it doesn't matter to her that I believe that. But it still matters to Quinn (more than she would like) that she gets to believe that herself.

It pulls me back to my conversation with Nicholas in the hotel suite last night—to the thing he didn't want to admit. That moment that Nicholas let me know the organization was behind what happened to Kate on the side of the road.

Quinn is just as uncomfortable as I am to be going back to that moment because she knows that she can't deny that. It doesn't matter if she's managed to convince herself that it was an accident—that Kate's death wasn't the intended result that afternoon. It doesn't even matter if that's true.

In one way or another, she and her family are the reason Kate died. In one way or another, all our fates were sealed when she did.

"Anyway," Quinn says. "I don't know what you think you're driving toward here. That I should stop holding your husband responsible? That I'm the one who could've made a different choice?"

I consider what's on that tablet, which impacts all of Quinn's siblings who, either by action or inaction, tried making a different

The First Time I Saw Him

choice. It didn't get any of them far enough away from where they started.

"I was actually going to say the opposite," I say. "I was going to say that we all have fewer choices than we'd like. And your choice now, mine too, is down to just one. The same choice, really. For both of us."

"And what's that?"

"To end this," I say. "Here."

She pauses, as if considering that. And I know that, despite her posturing, she hears what I'm saying. She has to hear what I'm saying. There's a tablet full of reasons why her future depends on her hearing what I'm saying. That this is our last chance to do it—both of us. It's our last chance to leave the past in the past, once and for all.

We have this in common. It may be the only thing we have in common. We have both spent our lives trying not to be at the mercy of what came before us. Trying, against the odds, to get our families to somewhere better.

"Maybe . . ." she says. "Maybe, that's true for me and you. But nothing just ends. Not in this family."

That stops me. "What do you mean by that?"

"I mean, there's always a cost," she says. "You get that by now, don't you? When you come for my family, there's always a cost."

There's always a cost. She holds on to the word *cost*, like a secret she's not sure she will let me in on.

It would be easy to think that Quinn is simply trying to scare me—that she is trying to make me think that, even now, when she has no cards, she is still playing a game I don't understand.

But it doesn't feel like a bluff. It feels like the truth.

There's always a cost. What will the cost of this be? It won't be to me and Bailey. It can't be. Owen has ensured that it won't be to us. Quinn, despite herself, confirming the same.

She holds my gaze, not blinking, not turning away. But I turn away from her, looking down at the cliffs below, the whole of Èze stretching out below. The cliffs and the houses. Frank's house. Her father's house.

I can feel her eyes still on me. But I keep my eyes on those cliffs, giving myself a moment to process, to figure out what she wants me to hear in what she's not yet saying. And so I don't give it away—how deeply that's penetrating. Her threat. Her threat that sounds less like a threat and more like a fact. *There's always a cost.*

If it won't be us, then what will it be? A loud thumping in my ear, in my heart, in my shoulder. Where his wound is. Nicholas's wound.

Because I start to know the answer. The answer inside this question: Will it be to Nicholas?

With all the talk today of our safety, not once did anyone discuss his safety. Not once was Nicholas mentioned.

And it starts to coalesce for me. There is always a cost when you come for this family. Nicholas would know this. He would know this better than anyone.

Of course, this would be the trade Nicholas is most willing to make, knowing he doesn't have much time left. Isn't that the trade he would willingly make, even if he had all the time in the world?

Nicholas would still make that trade for Bailey. We would all make that trade, without a moment's hesitation, for our children.

I turn in the direction of the back room—toward those windows we can't see through. Quinn's eyes following mine. She is as worried as I am about what is happening with Nicholas and her father. Maybe for different reasons, but worried all the same: her fate is as locked up as mine in what is happening in that room.

The First Time I Saw Him

This is when I realize something else. Or perhaps, I should say, when I realize *someone* else. Someone else who is involved in this. Someone else who, not unlike Nicholas, is willing to do what needs to be done to protect his children. Someone who would protect his children, even from themselves.

It hits me, like a bomb. The throbbing in my jaw. My heartbeat coming in behind it. The inside of that back room. All of it spinning together. Because I know it. Suddenly and irrevocably.

I know it, as sure as I've ever known anything: It isn't just Owen and Nicholas who are behind this.

One Year Ago

"I was a little surprised to hear from you," Frank said. "To be honest."

"I'm sure."

Frank and Nicholas were in Nicholas's office at The Sanctuary, Nicholas's lake house out in Texas Hill Country. They were having late-afternoon drinks, just the two of them. The sun was going down over the lake, the early evening air placid and welcoming. The world around them, for the moment, easy.

"Should I not have reached out?" Nicholas asked.

"No. Of course. I'm glad you did."

Nicholas topped off Frank's whiskey, taking a seat on the couch across from him. It was strange being back in this room, having a drink with his oldest friend. Strange and also eerily normal—eerily familiar. It was almost like they were back where they belonged, sitting here together. Because, in a way, they were.

"Well . . ." Nicholas said. "When I read about Bradley's wedding, it seemed like it was time . . ."

Frank forced a smile, but Nicholas could see it. Frank was showing restraint. Nicholas could read it in Frank's face. He could imagine everything Frank wanted to say: That it was past time. That it had pained him, every day, the way they had parted. That Nicholas was, to this day, the only real friend Frank had ever had. Didn't that count for something? If it couldn't count for everything, didn't it get to count for something?

"It's pretty wild, wouldn't you say?" Frank finally said. "Bradley meeting a young woman from Midland, let alone marrying her?"

Nicholas shook his head, letting out a small laugh. What were the odds? Bradley was marrying a young woman from Texas. A young woman who grew up less than a hundred miles from where Jenny, Bradley's own mother, grew up—less than a hundred miles from where Nicholas himself grew up. A young woman (a high school English teacher) who, from what Nicholas was gathering from Frank, was a lot like Jenny had been. Lovely and kind and smart. As honest as they come.

Nicholas understood why Frank found it crazy, but it just felt to Nicholas like more proof—did he need more proof at this point?—that as far away as we try to get, we end up where we start.

"The wedding's going to be in Midland next month," Frank said. "Big ballroom wedding at her parents' country club. It's going to be awful, I'm sure. Cold chicken dinners and a dessert buffet. Ten-piece band that can't play for shit. But lots of whiskey. Would love to have you there to help get me through it."

"You may want to hold on that invitation."

"And why is that?"

Nicholas didn't answer, not at first. He took a long sip of his own drink, bracing himself. Bracing himself for what he was about to do—what he was about to do for insurance. The ultimate insurance that he could get his family the safety they deserved.

"There's someone I need you to meet, Frank."

"Okay . . ." Frank put his drink down, suddenly on higher alert.

Which is when Owen walked through the door.

"Are you out of your fucking mind?"

"I'm going to need that favor now, Frank," Nicholas said.

Old Friends

"Did you have to shoot me?" Nicholas asks.

They are sitting at the corner table, a first aid kit between them. Frank is working on Nicholas's shoulder. He is tending carefully to the wound, applying alcohol and cream, a sterilized bandage.

"It felt like the moment called for it," Frank says.

"Did it?"

"You'll be fine. I barely grazed you."

"Oh good. So nothing to worry about."

Frank lets out a small laugh, meeting Nicholas's gaze. Then he turns back to the wound, taking a final look at how he's sealed it.

"That dressing should hold until tomorrow. Maybe forty-eight hours. Maybe. But you'll need a real doctor at some point."

"No kidding."

Nicholas puts his jacket back on, gingerly, taking a deep breath—his arm heavy and leaden. His phone starting to buzz in his pocket, against his skin. His phone, which has probably been buzzing.

Nicholas is running late. They're well over the twenty-minute mark. Nicholas and Hannah both are out of time here.

"Is that him?" Frank asks.

"Probably."

Nicholas doesn't have to ask who Frank is talking about. He knows that Frank thinks it's Owen.

And he sees Frank turn that over in his head—Frank who is still so uncomfortable with this. Owen, for so long, on the other side of the line from them. Owen, who could end up on the other side of the line again if he calls in the police, which may just happen if Nicholas doesn't leave here now. If Nicholas doesn't end this himself.

Nicholas understands that. He feels it in his own skin. How, despite all the planning, this won't begin to feel better, not until he and Hannah are gone from here. Not when Frank could still change his mind about his part. They need him for his part. For the insurance of it all. That, after tonight, Hannah will be safe moving forward, with Bailey. And with Owen.

"I should go," Nicholas says. "He's not going to wait much longer."

"Well, he's going to have to wait just a little longer, isn't he?"

"Frank, come on."

"Look, I know you don't want to go through this again, but . . ."

"You're going to go through it again?"

"They're going to demand a sacrifice on some level, Nick," Frank says. "They'll be suspicious if I don't demand a sacrifice on some level."

"We've gone through this."

Frank ignores this, keeps talking through, as much for himself as for Nicholas. "Then you know as well as I do that this won't end here, not for you. It can't. You must know that. I can't protect you from it. You knew that, showing up here today."

"I'm aware."

And Nicholas was aware, of course. Tonight's delivery has sealed it. It has sealed what Owen and Nicholas most needed sealed. Quinn and Teddy won't ever go after the kids again. No one in the organization will. They can't. There will be no bomb under a car one day. No men around every corner, not anymore. Because it will seal their fates too. And they are nothing, Quinn and Teddy, if not self-interested. They are interested in protecting themselves first and foremost.

The First Time I Saw Him

But they're also interested in punishing someone for putting them in that position. That someone, this time, will be Nicholas.

"I don't understand you doing this, Nicky . . ." Frank pauses. "Not for him."

"It's not for him."

"You sure about that?"

Nicholas starts to answer, but then he thinks better of it. Because it's beside the point. The point is what's best for Bailey. Bailey and Hannah. That's his primary concern—and Owen coming home is good for them. Bailey needs a father again. Hannah deserves her husband. And, if Nicholas is being honest, Owen has earned some relief. For the last five years, Owen did everything to keep Bailey safe. He did everything to ensure Hannah's and Bailey's safety long-term.

But even if he hadn't, if none of those things were true, would it matter? Wouldn't Nicholas be here anyway? We do what we need to do for our children—and they are all his children. Owen belongs to him too, after all.

Which brings Nicholas to it. What this is all really about—what he should tell Frank and what he can't tell him, what he can't say out loud, not to anyone.

That Nicholas still dreams of his daughter every night—every single night. He still dreams of that day he found Kate on the side of the road. He plays it over and over again, on a relentless loop, that moment when he found her.

He and Bailey had just left the park and Bailey was asleep in the stroller—the only blessing of this was that Bailey was asleep in that stroller. Nicholas assumed Kate was running late and so he'd just left her a voicemail that they were leaving the park and they would meet her at her house. That she should take her time. That they were doing great.

Then he turned the corner, and he saw Kate splayed out, halfway down the block. Her body, his daughter's body, was half on the curb, half off it—her head and shoulders in the street, her legs twisted out in an unnatural direction.

And, still, before he got to her—before Nicholas bent down beside her and turned her over—he got to believe it. He got to believe his daughter was okay. That she had been in some sort of accident. That she was hurt, but she was okay.

He was her father. He raced down the street toward his kid with that one, unshakable thought: He was her father and he would do all the things that needed to be done so his daughter was okay again.

Then he touched her.

And there was no story he could tell himself to make anything better, not anymore, not ever again.

Nicholas never really left her there. He never left the side of that road. The rest of his life—the glorious and miserable rest of it all—has all been details.

Nicholas offers Frank a small smile, a sad smile. "Didn't think you'd make it to eighty, Frank."

"Who did?"

Nicholas stands up, taps Frank on the shoulder, like Morse code. Like a reminder that he needs to go now. Right now. Or Owen will have the police in here. He'll have them in here, escorting them all out.

"It was smart of you to bring her with you tonight," Frank says. "It was smart to bring Hannah."

"No, that wasn't me. She insisted on coming. I tried to stop her."

"Either way, it helps," he says. "I don't have to find a reason to argue the point with my kids that tonight is not the moment to settle up on all of this. Even my kids aren't dumb enough to want a witness..."

Nicholas nods. He knows that what Frank is saying is true. Quinn and Teddy can't touch Hannah—that's the deal now. She gets to be

The First Time I Saw Him

safe, just like Frank's children are safe. They can't keep her from walking out of here tonight, even if they want to. And by extension, because Hannah was brave enough to come with Nicholas, they won't stop him from walking out of here either. No one, especially in this family, wants a witness.

Still, Nicholas wishes she hadn't made that choice. Nicholas is not particularly invested in his own safety, not at this point. He's invested in Bailey, only in Bailey, and her having a future with both of her parents, safe and together.

Bailey having exactly the life she deserves—that's really all that Nicholas is interested in.

"Just do me a favor, Nick," Frank says. "Go somewhere I don't know about."

"There's nowhere you don't know about."

"I hope that's not true."

Nicholas can only shrug, straighten his back. It's true and it's not that Frank doesn't know about the place where Nicholas is going. After all, he's sure that Meredith mentioned the farm in Tuscany to Jenny at some point—the farm where Meredith's grandmother grew up. Did Meredith also mention it to Frank? Nicholas can't be sure. But it would've been fifteen years ago now. Longer.

Frank doesn't know that Nick's wife was buried there, Kate beside her. One way or another, now, Nicholas will be buried there too.

Frank stands up. He stands up and moves close to Nicholas. And they take each other in for the last time. One of them at eighty, the other not too far behind, but knowing he won't reach that same fate.

That's not in the cards now. If he gets this one miracle, it's too much to also hope for the other.

Nicholas knows this is probably why Frank can't seem to let it go—why Frank feels the need to take one more shot at convincing him. As if Frank doesn't already know that it's a fool's errand—as if there is anything he can do to change anything about what's going to happen now. As if what Frank is doing (what they're both doing here, together) isn't actually something else. Something closer to saying goodbye.

"It's not too late, Nick," he says. "Don't trade your life for his."

Nicholas puts out his hand and reaches toward his oldest friend, their lives, their fates linked—the way you are linked to the people who know you best, whatever time and distance you put between you, whatever break you try to make.

"Didn't you hear, Frank?" he says. "I'm already dead."

And, forty-three years too late, Nicholas walks away.

Seventy-Two Hours Ago

"I owe you an apology," Nicholas said.

"We're past all that now," Owen said.

"Are we though?"

Owen looked away.

Nicholas wanted to push it, force the conversation, but he stopped himself. There was no point in trying to litigate any of this further. What did Nicholas expect Owen to say anyway?

It was ironic in a way: for so long his son-in-law blamed Nicholas for what happened to Kate. But, now that they were on the other side of it, Owen just wanted Nicholas to stop blaming himself. And here was Nicholas—only wanting the same for Owen. Right or wrong didn't matter. None of it mattered. Wasn't that love, after all? Wasn't that forgiveness? At the end of the day, I want you to be free.

"You don't owe me that," Owen said. "Not anymore."

"You look worried though."

"I just keep coming back to it," Owen said.

"To Hannah?" Nicholas asked.

Owen nodded. "She knows I'd never allow her to be in harm's way."

"She knows I wouldn't allow it either."

"What are you going to do?" Owen said. "When she figures it out?"

"I'm going to say goodbye."

The Good Lawyer Is Free

"You should have told me," I say.

"Hannah, not here," Nicholas says. "Not anywhere near here."

We are walking at a fast clip down the cobblestone path, away from the hotel—back down the steps, which are taking us past the Nietzsche Path, out of the main village. Away from all this.

The municipal police follow ten yards behind. A strange, silent escort. It doesn't seem like anyone is following behind them, but we wouldn't know, would we? We wouldn't know for sure, not yet. The shadowy figures have been following me too long for me to trust they're no longer following me still.

So I don't say anything else. Neither of us says anything again until we are down those steps, leading out of the village and down the hill, the hotel far behind us.

Then it's Nicholas who speaks first. He leans in toward me, keeping his voice low.

"It would have been far too risky to clue you in to Frank's involvement ahead of time," Nicholas says. "Plus, I needed to see if you bought it. So I could judge whether Quinn and Teddy bought it too."

They did buy it—I am sure. Quinn wasn't focused on what her father knew. She was focused on her own safety. Her safety, and her family's safety. She was subsumed by it. She and Teddy both were now.

It's nice to not be alone in that—to not be alone in the rest of it either. We will be okay now. Bailey and I both will. We will be okay, if we are careful.

"I just . . . I'm trying to understand . . ." I pause, trying to move myself closer to what's getting to me. "Why would Frank move against his own family?"

"He doesn't see it like that," Nicholas says. "He's shoring them up for the loopholes they seem to keep missing. The bad decisions they keep making. And he trusts that I'm not going to hurt his family, not without provocation. I've organized my life to avoid it. He's just giving me the leverage to make sure they don't hurt mine."

I nod because I understand that part. I understand how he could convince himself he's doing something else. But the part I don't understand is what I feel in my gut—Quinn's words pushing around in my head like a current. In my heart.

There's always a cost.

"But what about you?" I say. "What happens to you now?"

"We've been through this," he says. "You know what happens now."

"That wasn't my question. You heard my question. What happens to *you* now, Nicholas?"

I turn and watch him, waiting for him to speak. If the answer is that he is coming with us, he would readily volunteer it. If it is that he is going back to Austin, he'd offer that up too. But he says nothing. He says nothing and keeps his eyes straight ahead as we turn into the parking lot, the car coming into view. Our car and the small police station and the road that will lead me out of here. That will lead me to Bailey. To Owen. The pounding in my jaw is worse though. Worse when it should be better.

"You don't get out of this, do you?"

He doesn't answer me. But I do the math anyway. I do the math on what is happening back at that party. Frank is walking his family through our delivery—the tablet, the documents—as if they need to walk through it. They all know that they don't have a choice, not anymore. All of Nicholas's family gets left alone, forever now—or Quinn and Teddy will seal their own fate as well.

Except for this. When they demand a price for this level of betrayal, Frank will echo that demand. He will demand Nicholas. And they'll start going about it, all the ways they can try to get to him.

"I wouldn't have agreed to this," I say. "Not if I had known you'd be in danger."

"Why do you think I didn't tell you?"

He is trying to be light, but I don't feel light. I feel heavy.

And I see it—the blood soaking through his shirt, the bandage beneath it, sticking to his neck and his skin.

"I'm serious, Nicholas."

"Then be serious about the right part," he says. "I walked out of there tonight because you insisted on coming with me. I owe you a thank-you for that."

I put my hand on his arm, gently. I put my hand below the wound. "You shouldn't be walking anywhere," I say. "You need a doctor."

Nicholas pulls the car keys out of his pocket, and hands them to me.

"What I need is for you to drive us," he says. "Away from here."

∼

"What do you want me to tell Bailey?" I say.

We're driving down the Moyenne Corniche, the winding road that will lead us toward Antibes. The world around us is stunning and quiet: the precipitous cliffs winding us past the historic Hotel Cap Estel, the Silva Maris Port—the Mediterranean Sea glistening as we move closer to where we're going.

"She thinks you're coming back to her . . ." I say. "She's counting on you coming back to her."

"So tell her I will be back," he says. "One way or another."

I turn and look at him. "I won't lie to her . . ."

"Then tell her the truth."

"Which is?"

"That I'm spending tonight driving down one of the most beautiful roads in the world with one of my favorite people. And I'm heading to one of my favorite places on this planet . . ." He pauses. "I'm happier than I've been in a long time. I really am. Tell her that. Tell her that I'm good for now."

"Nicholas . . ."

He reaches out, touches my hand. "Hannah. I'll take now."

He looks at me, but he doesn't have to say it. This is a bargain he's happy to make. He would have given up more than that for one more day with his daughter. For the last day that he just got with mine. He would give them both everything he had. So would Owen. So did Owen. They had that in common.

Nicholas turns toward the window, and we are quiet, both of us, because suddenly there is too much to say. Too much to say, and not enough time.

I drive into downtown Antibes, into the city center, and turn down a side street, pulling into the parking garage. I drive toward the spot in the corner where the other car is waiting—the car Owen left here.

The engine is running. Seth is sitting in the driver's seat. And two people, dressed exactly like us—the woman in a black dress, and the man in the same sports jacket—are waiting in the back seat.

In a moment, I'll hand them the keys to this car and they'll get

The First Time I Saw Him

into it and pull out of the parking lot and head down the highway toward the airport in Nice.

Just in case they are following us, we will give them someone else to follow. They can follow them back to that airport in Nice, where Nicholas Bell is scheduled on the first morning flight back to America, ultimately landing him in Austin, Texas. A flight he will of course never get on.

His plan, both of our plans, leading us somewhere else. Nicholas will get into the car with Seth. Seth who will drive Nicholas the six hours to Tuscany. To tend to his wound. To walk with him around the farm where he will be now. Where he will be buried now. Where, for as long as possible, we can hope that he stays safe.

And I'll head out to the street here and take a short walk to the hotel three blocks over—where I'll get in a taxi to Old Town. To the marina. To where Bailey is waiting for me. And her father. Her grandfather made sure of it. The three of us will be together again and safe to be together again because of what he is willing to do here. What he has insisted on doing here. For his family.

"You know, maybe it's not my place . . ." I say.

"When has that stopped you before?"

I give him a smile. "You should try to forgive yourself, Nicholas, if you can. You deserve it."

"Come on, I . . ."

Nicholas starts to argue, but his voice catches in his throat and he just shakes his head. Because he can't hear that. Of course he can't. None of us can hear anyone else when—despite our best efforts, despite all evidence to the contrary—we still think we've failed our children.

"I think maybe that takes a bigger person than me."

"I don't know about that," I say. "I mean, at the end of the day, you've forgiven him, haven't you?"

"Owen?"

"Owen."

He tilts his head, back and forth, as if to say sort of. And we both laugh. I've come to love it. That laugh.

"Have you?" he asks.

For which part? I want to say. The list is long and involved, the way it gets to be when you've been apart longer than you've been together. I can cull it down to the few largest injuries, as if those encompass all of it, anyway. As if it's really possible to encompass what it means to have the person you love disappear (even if he had to); to leave you to relive the time you were together (as if it didn't count); for thinking your life was safe when it wasn't.

For the knowledge you carry now—that you will always carry now. That we're never safe, not when we love someone. That, one way or another, we're always waiting for someone to disappear.

Seth gets out of the car, nods toward Nicholas. He wants to get going. They need to get going.

Before they do, I want to try again to get through to him. I need to say it in a way that he will hear it. Because this may be my last chance. It may be my last chance to tell him what I've come to believe. About him. About Owen.

That maybe, at the end of the day, it's not even about forgiveness. Or, at least, it's not only about forgiveness. It's about something deeper than that. Deeper than any limited understanding of being angry or hurt or deceived. Deeper than any understanding we may have of what we've gotten right and wrong. It's about our effort. The effort is the thing, isn't it? What effort will you make to be forgiven?

The First Time I Saw Him

What effort will you keep making, regardless of the cost, to show up for the people who need you?

I put my hand on his forearm, hold him there. He puts his free hand on top of mine, his eyes bright with tears.

"We've got her," I say. "I promise you. We've got Bailey forever. And that's thanks to you."

"If you need something to tell Bailey . . ." he says. "Start with that."

He smiles at me, and waits for me to let go of him, which I don't do. I move closer to him instead.

He pulls back.

"Enough of this. Bailey's waiting for you," he says. "They both are."

"They can wait a little longer."

He laughs, that gentle laugh. Then he kisses me on the forehead, holding there for a second too long. Holding there for a second too long for me to forget what's really happening here. A final memory.

"I don't want to say goodbye to you," I say.

"So let's just agree then," Nicholas says. "This won't be goodbye."

Which is, somehow, when it is.

The Docks Lead You Home

The marina is quiet. The water, serene.

Many of the boats are dark and shut down for the night. But there are some that have their evening lights on.

I walk quickly down the docks, the lights helping to guide me. I'm anxious to get eyes on Bailey—and on Owen. But I slow down as I pass by those active boats: a couple having a late dinner on their deck, an older man drinking a bottle of beer, a family pulling their suitcases on board, ready to head out at first light.

It strikes me, all at once, the similarity so disorienting. It's almost like being back on the docks in Sausalito. What it felt like every night in Sausalito—the magic of passing all those floating homes on the way to mine.

And, suddenly, it's five years ago again. It's five years in the future. I am simply doing what I do every night. I'm walking the docks after a long day—all those floating homes (all these boats) carrying their life stories, their own private dreams that only this small piece of the sea will ever get to know.

I'm feeling it move through me. The sense of peace that the water gives. The peace and the quiet and the certainty. All of which comes for me and comes back to me. Because here I am again, doing it.

I'm walking the docks again—heading home, again. To them.

I know which boat I'm looking for before I even know that this is the boat I'm looking for. It's one of the first boats in the International

Yacht Club quay—large yachts far in the distance, the smaller deep-sea boats on the berths closer in.

It's the boat I know the most about. The same make and model of the boat in Santa Cruz. In Marina del Rey. The French-manufactured boat that I learned how to operate, so I'd be prepared to navigate it anywhere. Nicholas had shared this with Owen. He had shared it with him so that if tonight hadn't worked out the way we needed it to, we'd have the means to run. This time, the three of us, together.

But it had worked out, hadn't it? It had worked out enough that we don't need to run, not anymore. Together, we get to do something else.

Before I step on board, I take one last look around. I look out at the docks and the marina and the town just beyond. The hundreds of lives going on just beyond this: weddings and late-season tourists and someone (somewhere) saying a final goodbye to a person they won't get back.

It started on a dock. And that's where it ends.

The First Time I Saw Him

When I step on board, there is a creak, the teak deck sliding beneath my feet.

I slip off my shoes, feel the wood against my toes. It doesn't matter that it's late in the evening—that the boat is mostly dark. I know the shape of this entire boat by heart. I know where I'm going. My first thought is Bailey. I'm going straight to her. Let me see her. Let me have eyes on her face and her skin and her arms to know she is fine. To let her know that I am.

I head down to the three small cabins, and find her sleeping in the farthest one.

I find her sleeping on the bed, cuddled into the fetal position. There's a keyboard on the floor, an open notebook beside it, papers strewn about. Her clothes and her towel are crowded in a messy bunch, surrounding her work.

I kneel down on the floor, so we are face-to-face. And I touch the side of her face, my sweet girl. A flicker of recognition crossing her face, a half-smile.

"You're home," she says.

"I'm home," I say.

I hold my hand against her cheek, brushing my forehead against her forehead, her smile growing a little bigger. But really, she is still more asleep than awake. Her eyes not even opening completely.

Tomorrow, after she's had some rest (after we both have), I'll wake her to watch the sunrise with me. We'll take two hot mugs of coffee out to the top deck and watch a sunrise that, she will tell me, may just rival our favorite sunrise in Santa Monica.

And we'll have to get into all of it—all the rest of it. Her grandfather and the cost of this. Though I won't call it a cost. I'll call it a blessing. Because that, at this point, is who Nicholas gets to be.

But for now, I just watch her. My sleeping girl. Her face in the soft light, that flicker of a smile, my hand on her face, holding her there as she falls into a deeper sleep. A deeper rest than she's had in a long time.

I don't know how long I sit like that—a moment, or several. I'm there long enough to allow myself to believe it. Bailey gets to be okay. For good now.

Then I head back up the stairs, back up to the teak deck.

I head to the edge of the deck—the edge closest to the sea. The tears filling my eyes as I let myself take it in.

The sea stretched out wide before me, the Mediterranean glowing. Quite literally, glowing: The water and the light and the high moon turning a shade of purple that the world has never shown me before.

A first sign (as if I need a sign) that I'm exactly where I need to be.

Which is when I feel him come up behind me.

Owen, a few feet behind me.

My hand is on the boat's railing. My eyes still on the water. In a moment, he will speak. Soft, but strong. He'll make a joke about how he's hoping it's true that I can operate this boat because we have a long way to go, the three of us. And Bailey is already giving out orders. Of course she is. She has all sorts of ideas for this overdue time together.

She wants to go to the Amalfi Coast, to a small town that her

The First Time I Saw Him

grandfather told her about called Sant'Agata sui Due Golfi—where you can eat lemons whole and walk in the hills and forget it for a while. The cost of what it took to bring us there. *She's very focused on those lemons,* Owen will joke.

And it will make me laugh. It will make me laugh in a way that will also make me sad—just at the moment when I'm supposed to be happy. Isn't that how it goes? All of it bubbling up. Call it anger. Or hope. Or longing. Isn't it really a longing that we name in other ways?

A longing for everything we'll have to walk through together to get back to the place we left each other, as if there is getting back to it. Everything we'll have to walk through to get somewhere better.

What will somewhere better look like? It will become clearer once we're back in California, stepping gingerly together back into real life. A more permanent life. A safe life. There is a large piece of land with a vineyard and farmhouse and a beautiful old barn, not too far from downtown Los Alamos—not too far from Bailey in Venice.

Paperwork is waiting to be signed. Owen has become quite a winemaker, and he would love to continue. He'd love to continue in the vein he's been taught. Small batch wines. Biodynamic. Fruit forward. He'd love to do something with those five acres of vineyard. And, more than anything, he'd love to transform it together—the beautiful old barn that will be my dream workshop.

If I want that too. Only, of course, if I want that too.

Or I can be mad. I can be mad at him forever, now that I have the luxury to be mad. I can be mad forever, or I can allow myself to feel it, what I'm naturally starting to feel, the letting go coming in hot and quick.

What else is there to do? We let it go. If we are lucky enough, we get to do that. We get to believe that we deserve it.

But first there is this.

The moment you've imagined.

The moment you haven't let yourself imagine.

This purple light and our kid sleeping safely and the two of us. Always now, until we have to let go, the two of us.

So I do it. The only thing I want to do. I turn toward him.

"Hannah," he says.

Acknowledgments

I am sitting and writing these acknowledgments longhand, which is something I don't usually do. I've held Hannah Hall close for so long that I think I'm trying to slow down our goodbye. Thank you, first and foremost, to all of the readers who didn't want to say goodbye either. Thank you for reaching out to me, and for your beautiful notes, and for embracing Hannah and Bailey and Owen. This sequel is for you . . .

Suzanne Gluck, thank you for not blinking when I called to tell you that the final moment in the design center wasn't just an end, it was also a beginning. Thank you, as always, for saying the one thing that helped me concretize where I most wanted that beginning to go.

Marysue Rucci, five novels together and twenty-year-old me still pinches herself that she gets to have an editor who cares so deeply about every word and how they feel and how they need to move. Grateful to you, beyond measure.

My gratitude to the amazing team at Scribner: Stu Smith, Brianna Yamashita, Maya Rutherford, Clare Maurer, Colleen Nuccio, Jaya Miceli, and Emma Taussig; Jonathan Karp, your emails about each novel sit on my desk. How lucky I feel to say that about my publisher.

A special thank you to Selina Walker and her team at Century Books for the exceptional UK home; to the team at WME, Lane Kizziah, Laura Bonner, Ari Greenburg, and Matilda Forbes Watson; and to Liz Biber and Meredith O'Sullivan and the incredible team at Lede.

Acknowledgments

To Sylvie Rabineau, my love and gratitude for your guidance and friendship and for being you. I couldn't adore you more.

The research for this novel took me to Paris and the South of France and Florida and Hawaii and along the California coast. Thank you to the teams at La Réserve Paris, Hôtel Château de La Chèvre d'Or, Musée Picasso, Hualalai, and Gnoss Field Airport.

Thank you, Katherine Eskovitz, for the legal guidance; Michael Frankel for the sailing wisdom; and Harriet Selina for sharing her beautiful poem, "A Prayer for Future Us."

For early reads and other invaluable insight, thank you to: Allison Winn Scotch, KCS & SS, Stephanie & Zack Levinson, Emily Usher, Jonathan Tropper & Stephanie Abram, Liz Squadron, Kira Goldberg, Dana Forman, Amanda Brown, Dusty Thomason, Shauna Seliy, Ali Woodruff, Ashley Strumwasser, Wendy Merry, James Feldman, Angourie Rice, Emma Destrubé, and Brenda Serpas.

My enduring gratitude to Reese Witherspoon, Lauren Neustadter, Sarah Harden, and the team at Hello Sunshine. And to Jennifer Garner, Hannah herself, for caring about (and caring for) everything HH needed to find her way home.

To the Dave and Singer families, my wonderful friends, and the village of moms with whom I feel so lucky to raise our children. Thank you for forgiving me for leaving my keys everywhere I go (and I do mean everywhere) and for letting me feed you and for being the people I trust with my kid. I love you and am so grateful for you.

Acknowledgments

That brings me to you, Josh. I'm not sure where to start. You told me to pick up *The Last Thing He Told Me* when I'd put it away in a drawer. Thank you for that. Thank you for reading every word first and making me feel like they're going somewhere important. Thank you, more than anything, for being my person. Since the moment I met you, I've been your biggest fan. How blessed it makes me feel that you are mine.

Finally, to Jacob, my beautiful boy. The day we arrived in the South of France to research this novel, we went to the Picasso Museum in Antibes. You sat on the bench with me in front of *Ulysses and sirens* while I unlocked the happy ending I was moving toward. How do I thank you for that gift? To get to be the person who sits there with you? You are forever my sweetest miracle, and my happiest ending of all.

About the Author

Laura Dave is the No. 1 *New York Times* bestselling author of eight novels, including *The Last Thing He Told Me*, *The Night We Lost Him*, and *Eight Hundred Grapes*. She lives in Los Angeles with her husband and their son.